4341

D1243009

24|.5

6/12

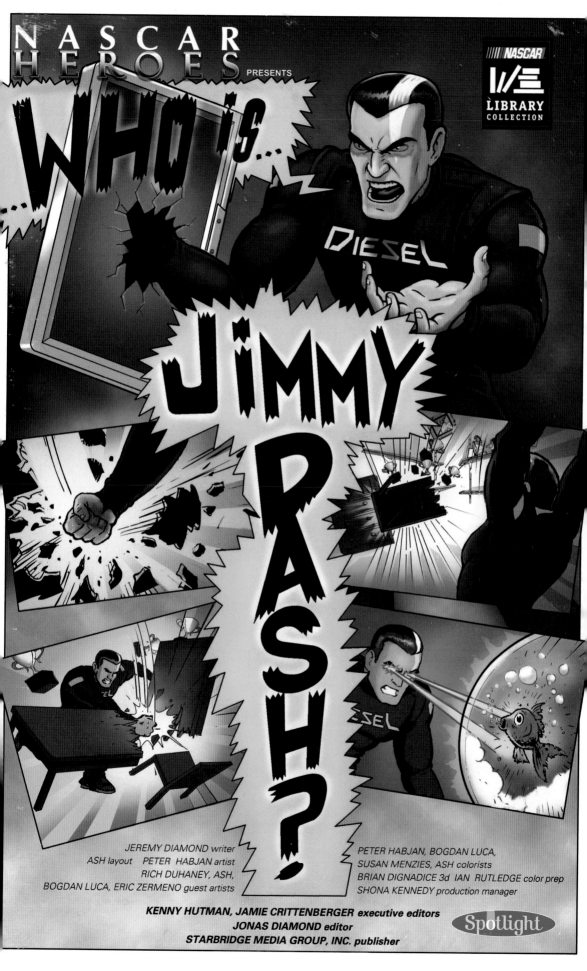

NASCAR HEROES PRESENTS
WHO IS... JIMMY RASH?

NASCAR LIBRARY COLLECTION

JEREMY DIAMOND writer
ASH layout   PETER HABJAN artist
RICH DUHANEY, ASH,
BOGDAN LUCA, ERIC ZERMENO guest artists

PETER HABJAN, BOGDAN LUCA,
SUSAN MENZIES, ASH colorists
BRIAN DIGNADICE 3d IAN RUTLEDGE color prep
SHONA KENNEDY production manager

KENNY HUTMAN, JAMIE CRITTENBERGER executive editors
JONAS DIAMOND editor
STARBRIDGE MEDIA GROUP, INC. publisher

Spotlight

VISIT US AT
www.abdopublishing.com

Reinforced library bound edition published in 2010 by Spotlight, a division of the ABDO Group, 8000 West 78th Street, Edina, Minnesota 55439. Spotlight produces high-quality reinforced library bound editions for schools and libraries. Published by agreement with Starbridge Media Group, Inc.

Library of Congress Cataloging-in-Publication Data

Diamond, Jeremy.
  Who is Jimmy Dash? / Jeremy Diamond, writer ; Peter Habjan, artist. -- Reinforced library bound ed.
    p. cm. -- (NASCAR heroes ; #2)
  "Nascar Library Collection."
  Summary: The radioactive accident that gave Dashiell James and his crew superpowers and turned him into Jimmy Dash, NASCAR driver, also transformed driver Jack Diesel into a superpowered archenemy who will do anything to stop Dash and learn his true identity.
  ISBN 978-1-59961-663-6
  1. Graphic novels. [1. Graphic novels. 2. Automobile racing--Fiction. 3. NASCAR (Association)--Fiction. 4. Superheroes--Fiction.] I. Habjan, Peter, ill. II. Title.
  PZ7.7.D52Who 2009
  741.5'973--dc22
                    2009009008

All Spotlight books have reinforced library bindings and
are manufactured in the United States of

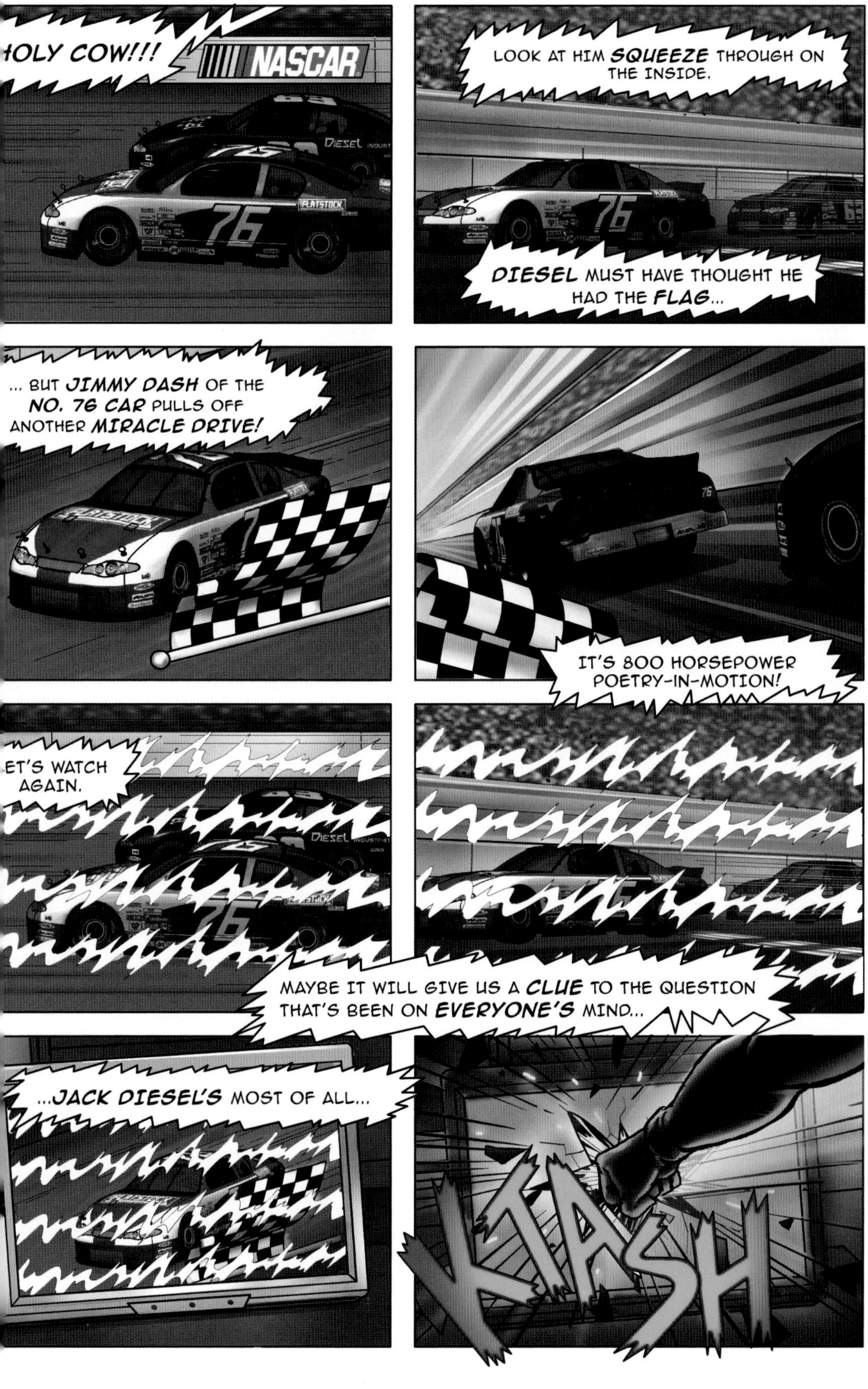

HOLY COW!!!
NASCAR
LOOK AT HIM SQUEEZE THROUGH ON THE INSIDE.
DIESEL MUST HAVE THOUGHT HE HAD THE FLAG...
... BUT JIMMY DASH OF THE NO. 76 CAR PULLS OFF ANOTHER MIRACLE DRIVE!
IT'S 800 HORSEPOWER POETRY-IN-MOTION!
LET'S WATCH AGAIN.
MAYBE IT WILL GIVE US A CLUE TO THE QUESTION THAT'S BEEN ON EVERYONE'S MIND...
...JACK DIESEL'S MOST OF ALL...
KRASH

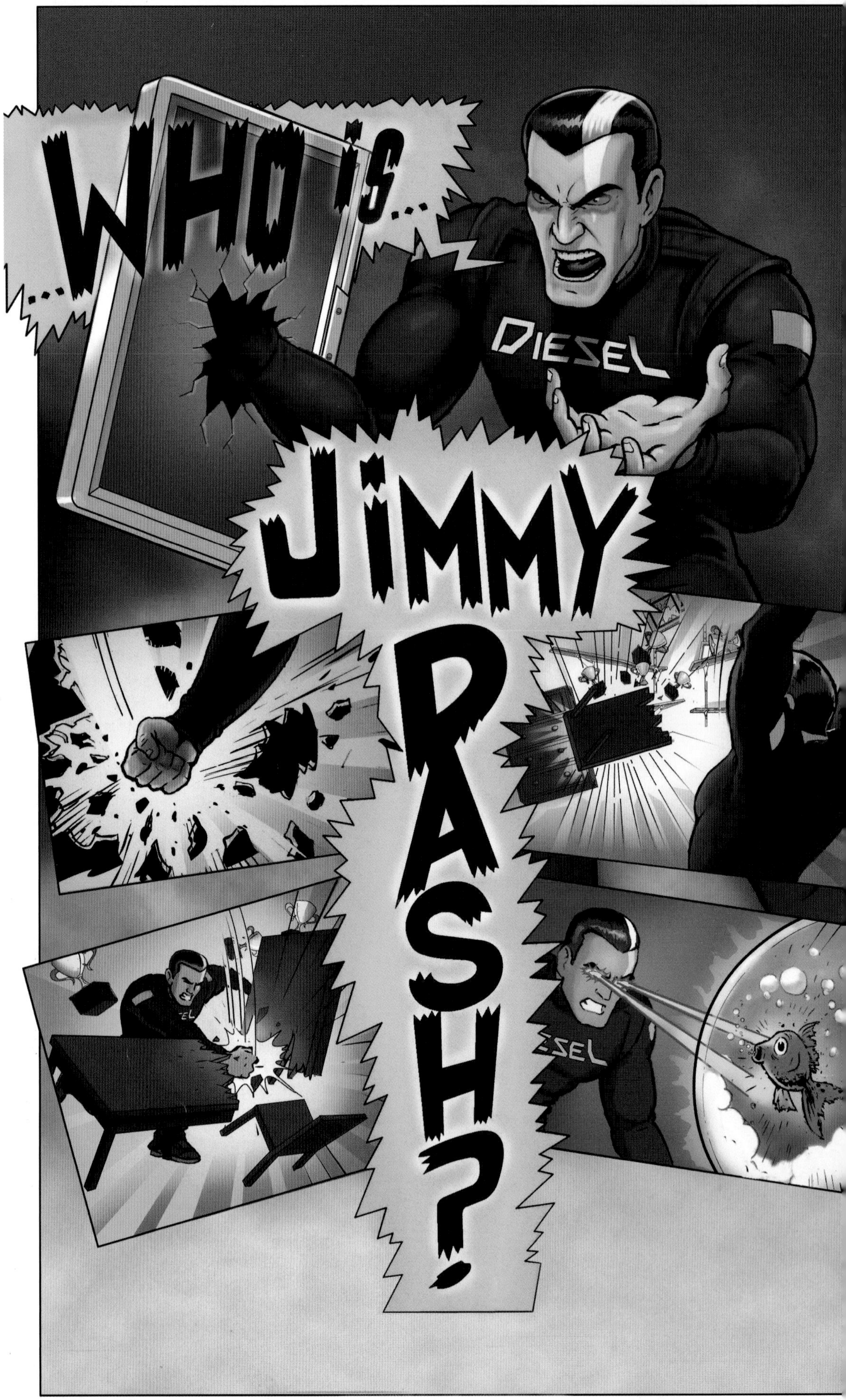
...WHO IS...
JIMMY RASH?
DIESEL

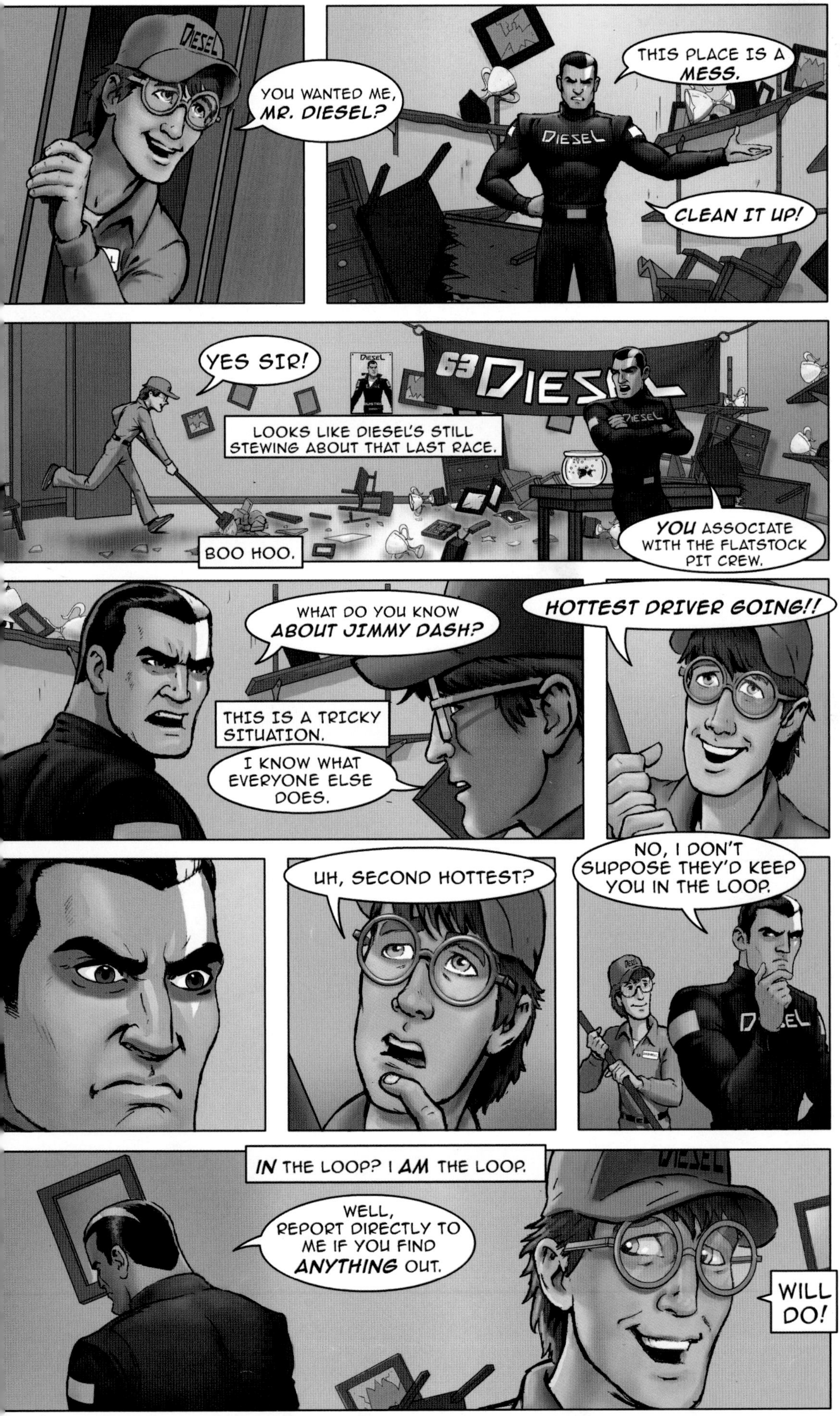
YOU WANTED ME, MR. DIESEL?
THIS PLACE IS A MESS.
CLEAN IT UP!
YES SIR!
LOOKS LIKE DIESEL'S STILL STEWING ABOUT THAT LAST RACE.
BOO HOO.
63 DIESEL
YOU ASSOCIATE WITH THE FLATSTOCK PIT CREW.
WHAT DO YOU KNOW ABOUT JIMMY DASH?
THIS IS A TRICKY SITUATION.
I KNOW WHAT EVERYONE ELSE DOES.
HOTTEST DRIVER GOING!!
UH, SECOND HOTTEST?
NO, I DON'T SUPPOSE THEY'D KEEP YOU IN THE LOOP.
IN THE LOOP? I AM THE LOOP.
WELL, REPORT DIRECTLY TO ME IF YOU FIND ANYTHING OUT.
WILL DO!

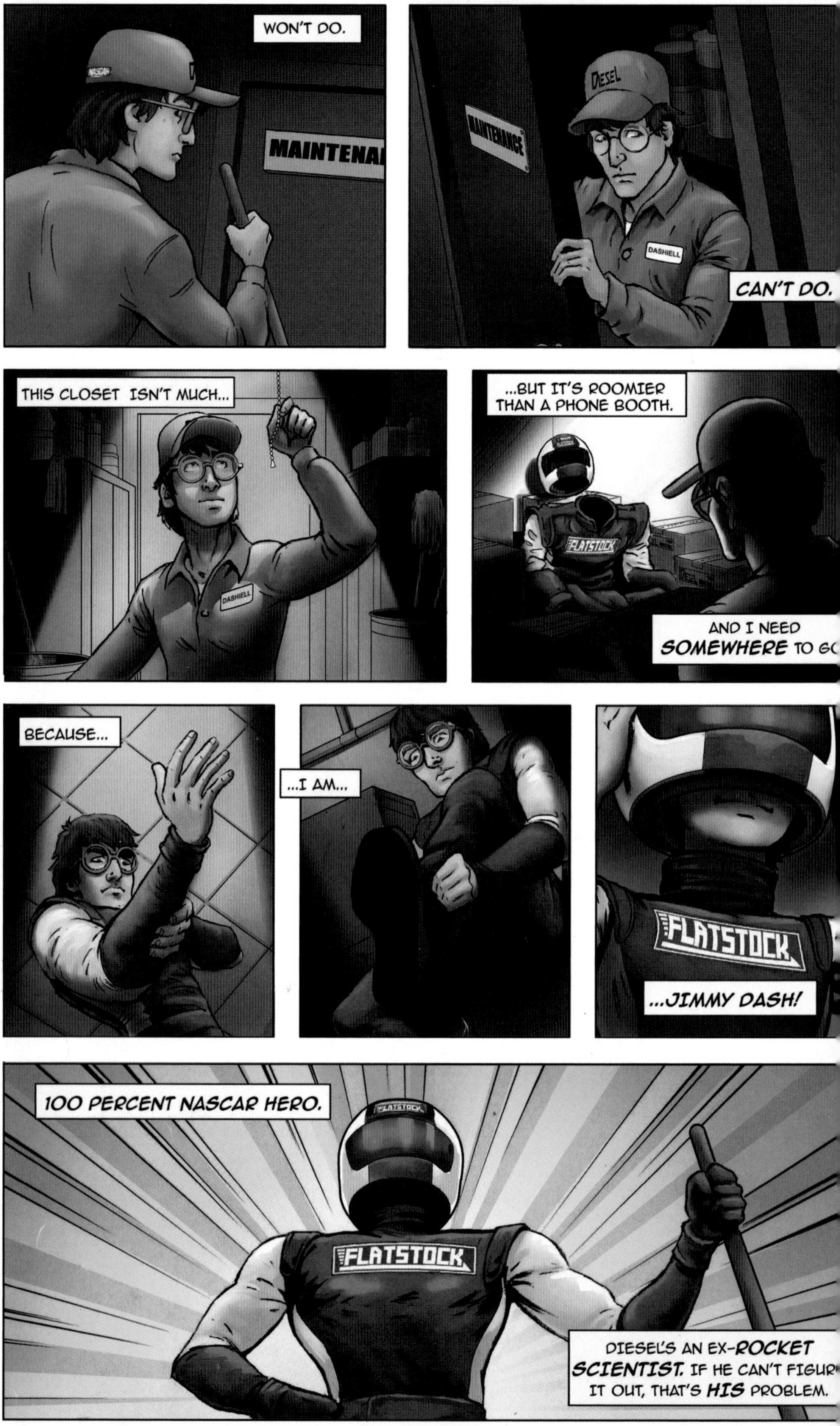

WON'T DO.
NASCAR
MAINTENAN
DIESEL
MAINTENANCE
DASHIELL
CAN'T DO.
THIS CLOSET ISN'T MUCH...
DASHIELL
...BUT IT'S ROOMIER THAN A PHONE BOOTH.
FLATSTOCK
AND I NEED SOMEWHERE TO GO
BECAUSE...
...I AM...
FLATSTOCK
...JIMMY DASH!
100 PERCENT NASCAR HERO.
FLATSTOCK
FLATSTOCK
DIESEL'S AN EX-ROCKET SCIENTIST. IF HE CAN'T FIGURE IT OUT, THAT'S HIS PROBLEM.

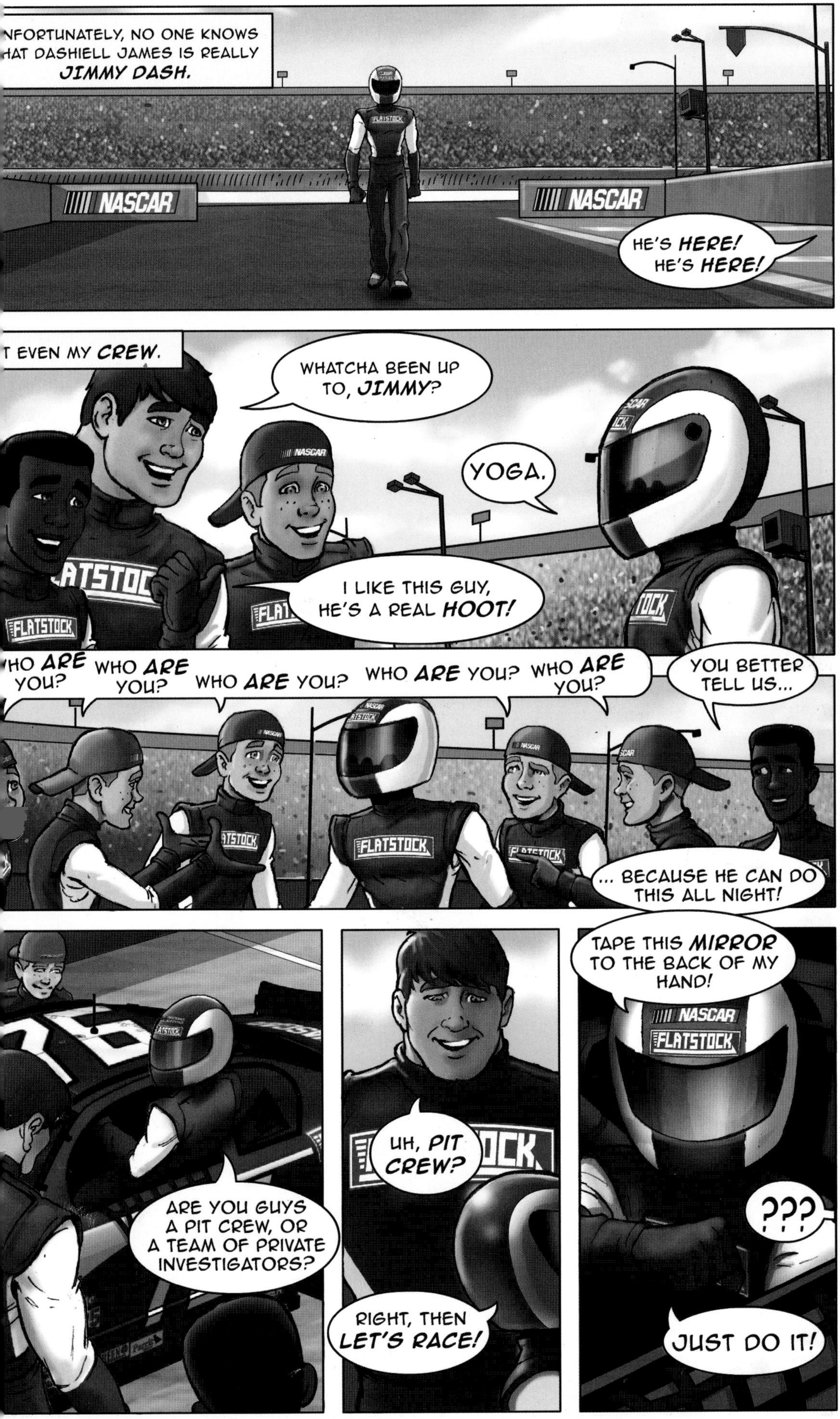
NFORTUNATELY, NO ONE KNOWS HAT DASHIELL JAMES IS REALLY JIMMY DASH.
HE'S HERE! HE'S HERE!
T EVEN MY CREW.
WHATCHA BEEN UP TO, JIMMY?
YOGA.
I LIKE THIS GUY, HE'S A REAL HOOT!
HO ARE YOU?
WHO ARE YOU?
WHO ARE YOU?
WHO ARE YOU?
WHO ARE YOU?
YOU BETTER TELL US...
... BECAUSE HE CAN DO THIS ALL NIGHT!
ARE YOU GUYS A PIT CREW, OR A TEAM OF PRIVATE INVESTIGATORS?
UH, PIT CREW?
RIGHT, THEN LET'S RACE!
TAPE THIS MIRROR TO THE BACK OF MY HAND!
???
JUST DO IT!

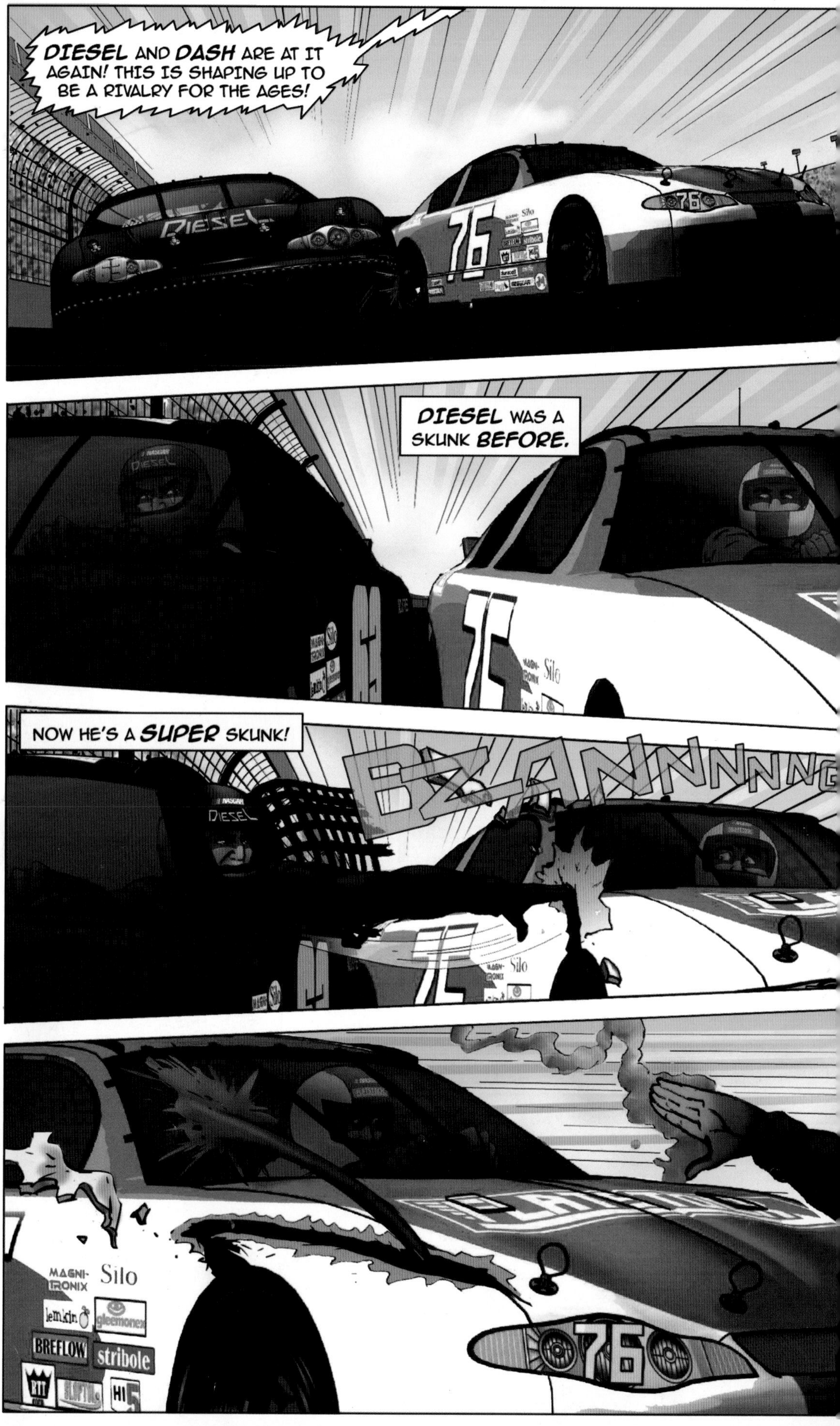
DIESEL AND DASH ARE AT IT AGAIN! THIS IS SHAPING UP TO BE A RIVALRY FOR THE AGES!
DIESEL WAS A SKUNK BEFORE.
NOW HE'S A SUPER SKUNK!
BZANNNNNG
DIESEL
76
Silo
MAGNI-TRONIX
stribole
BREFLOW
HI5

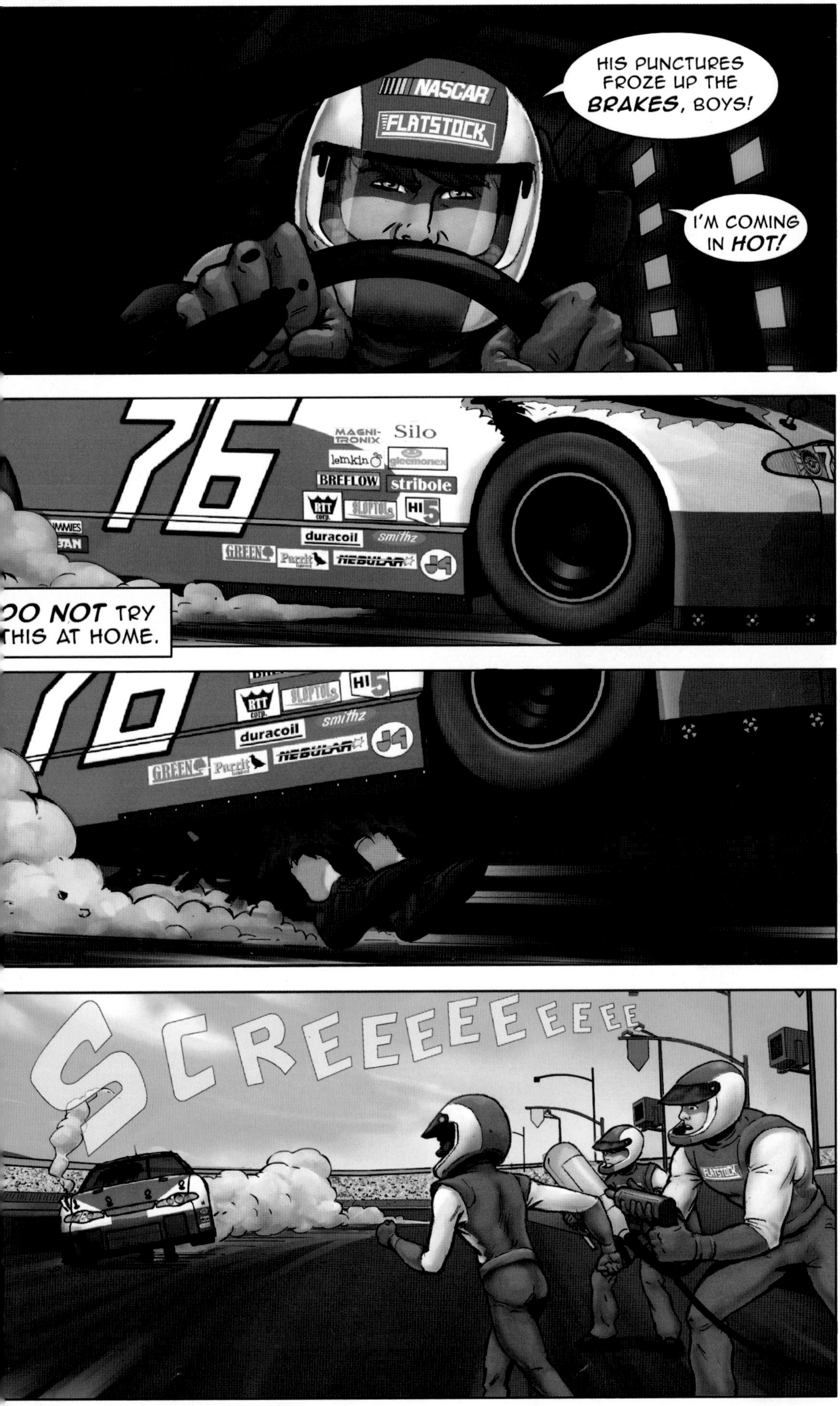
HIS PUNCTURES FROZE UP THE BRAKES, BOYS!
I'M COMING IN HOT!
DO NOT TRY THIS AT HOME.
SCREEEEEEEEE

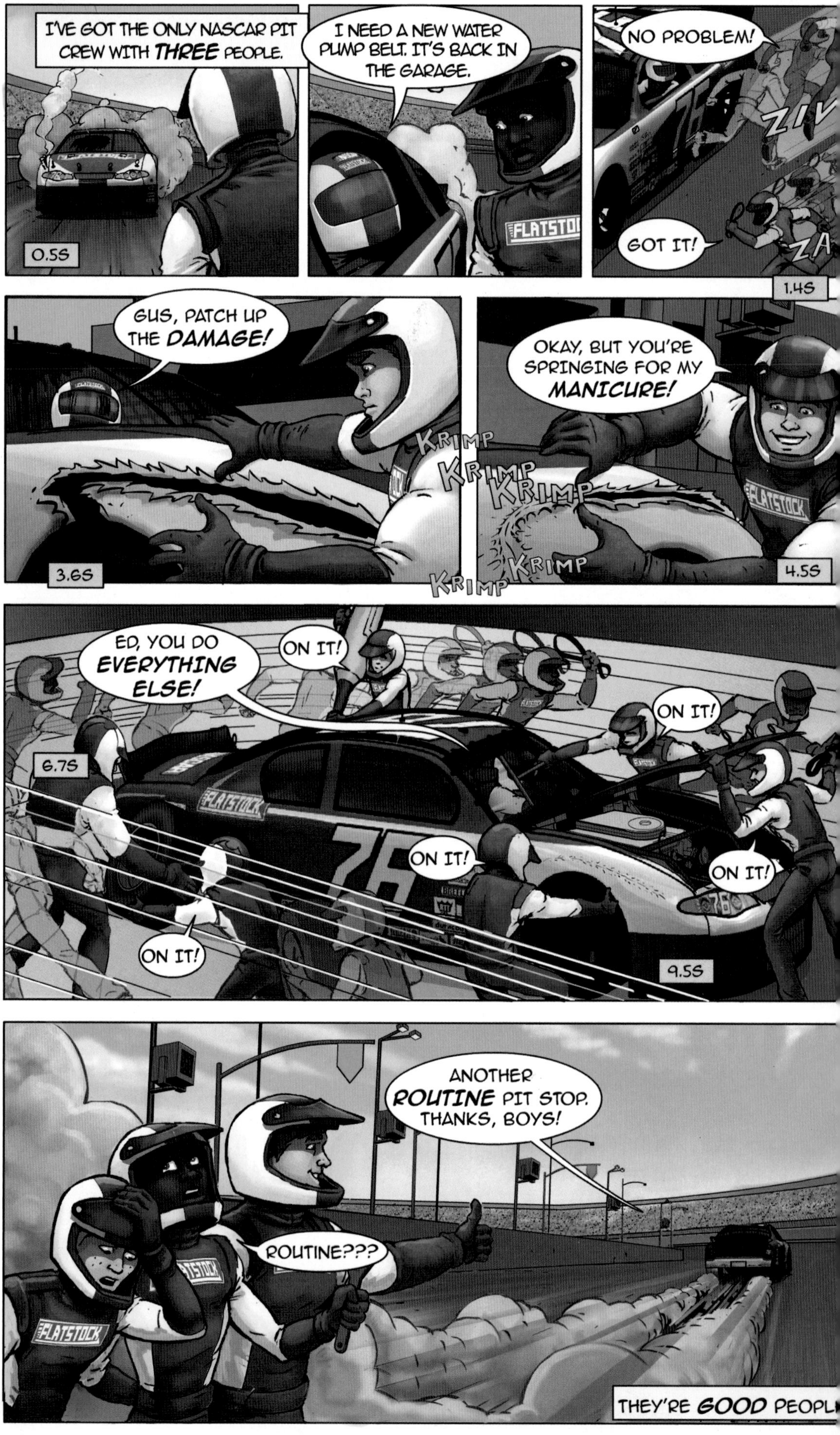
I'VE GOT THE ONLY NASCAR PIT CREW WITH THREE PEOPLE.
0.5S
I NEED A NEW WATER PUMP BELT. IT'S BACK IN THE GARAGE.
NO PROBLEM!
GOT IT!
1.4S
GUS, PATCH UP THE DAMAGE!
3.6S
KRIMP KRIMP KRIMP KRIMP KRIMP
OKAY, BUT YOU'RE SPRINGING FOR MY MANICURE!
4.5S
ED, YOU DO EVERYTHING ELSE!
ON IT!
6.7S
ON IT!
ON IT!
ON IT!
ON IT!
9.5S
ANOTHER ROUTINE PIT STOP. THANKS, BOYS!
ROUTINE???
THEY'RE GOOD PEOPL

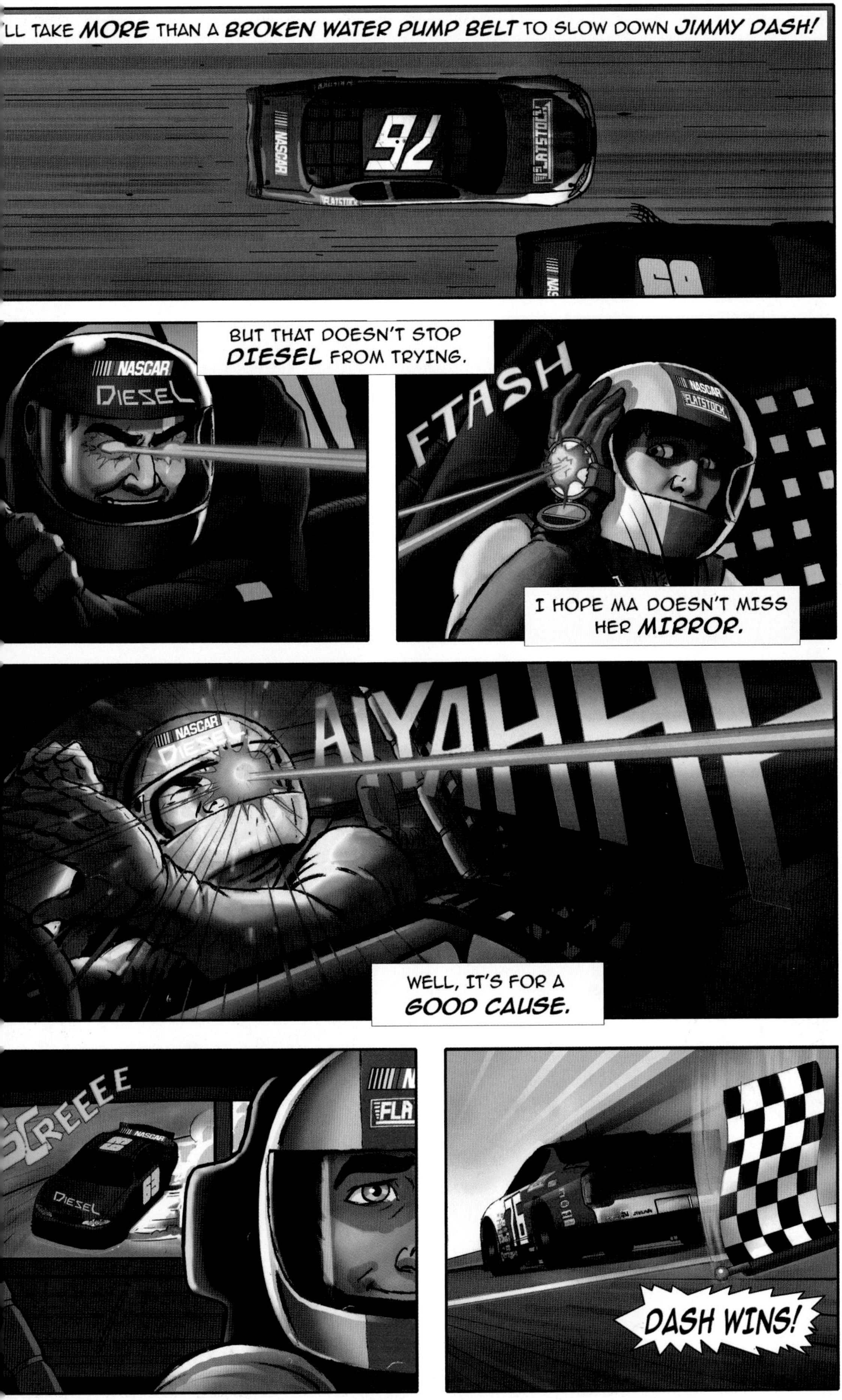
'LL TAKE MORE THAN A BROKEN WATER PUMP BELT TO SLOW DOWN JIMMY DASH!
BUT THAT DOESN'T STOP DIESEL FROM TRYING.
FTASH
I HOPE MA DOESN'T MISS HER MIRROR.
AIYAHHH
WELL, IT'S FOR A GOOD CAUSE.
SCREEEE
DASH WINS!

WUPPA WUPPA WUPPA

NICE RUN, JIMMY!

THANKS, BOSS!

BUT I HAVE **NO** TIME TO CELEBRATE.

I GOTTA GO!

SURE! GO **YOGA** SOME MORE!

WHERE THE HECK'S HE GOING?

coil

AND HOW THE HECK DID I GET **HOLES** IN THE FLOOR OF MY CAR?

FLATSTOCK

NO TIME TO PLAY **HERO**.

NANCE

TENANCE

I GOTTA GO **CLEAN** DIESEL'S OFFICE.

SUPER POWERS SUR DO COME IN HANDY

DIESEL

JUST IN TIME, TOO.

SLAM

DIESEL

HOW WAS THE **RACE** SIR?

GET **OUT!**

DIESEL

GOTTA GO

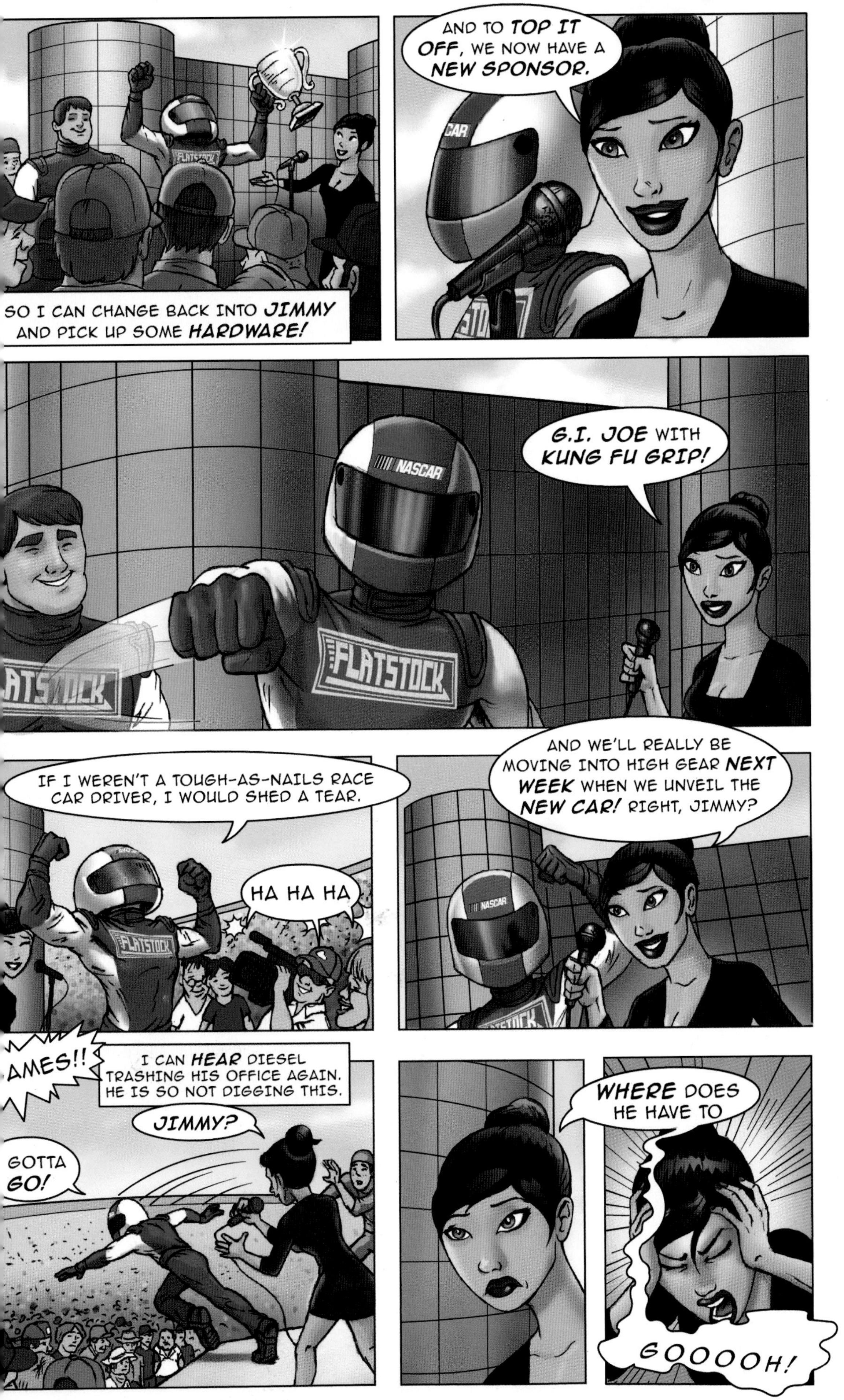
SO I CAN CHANGE BACK INTO JIMMY AND PICK UP SOME HARDWARE!
AND TO TOP IT OFF, WE NOW HAVE A NEW SPONSOR.
G.I. JOE WITH KUNG FU GRIP!
IF I WEREN'T A TOUGH-AS-NAILS RACE CAR DRIVER, I WOULD SHED A TEAR.
HA HA HA
AND WE'LL REALLY BE MOVING INTO HIGH GEAR NEXT WEEK WHEN WE UNVEIL THE NEW CAR! RIGHT, JIMMY?
AMES!!
I CAN HEAR DIESEL TRASHING HIS OFFICE AGAIN. HE IS SO NOT DIGGING THIS.
JIMMY?
GOTTA GO!
WHERE DOES HE HAVE TO
GOOOOOH!

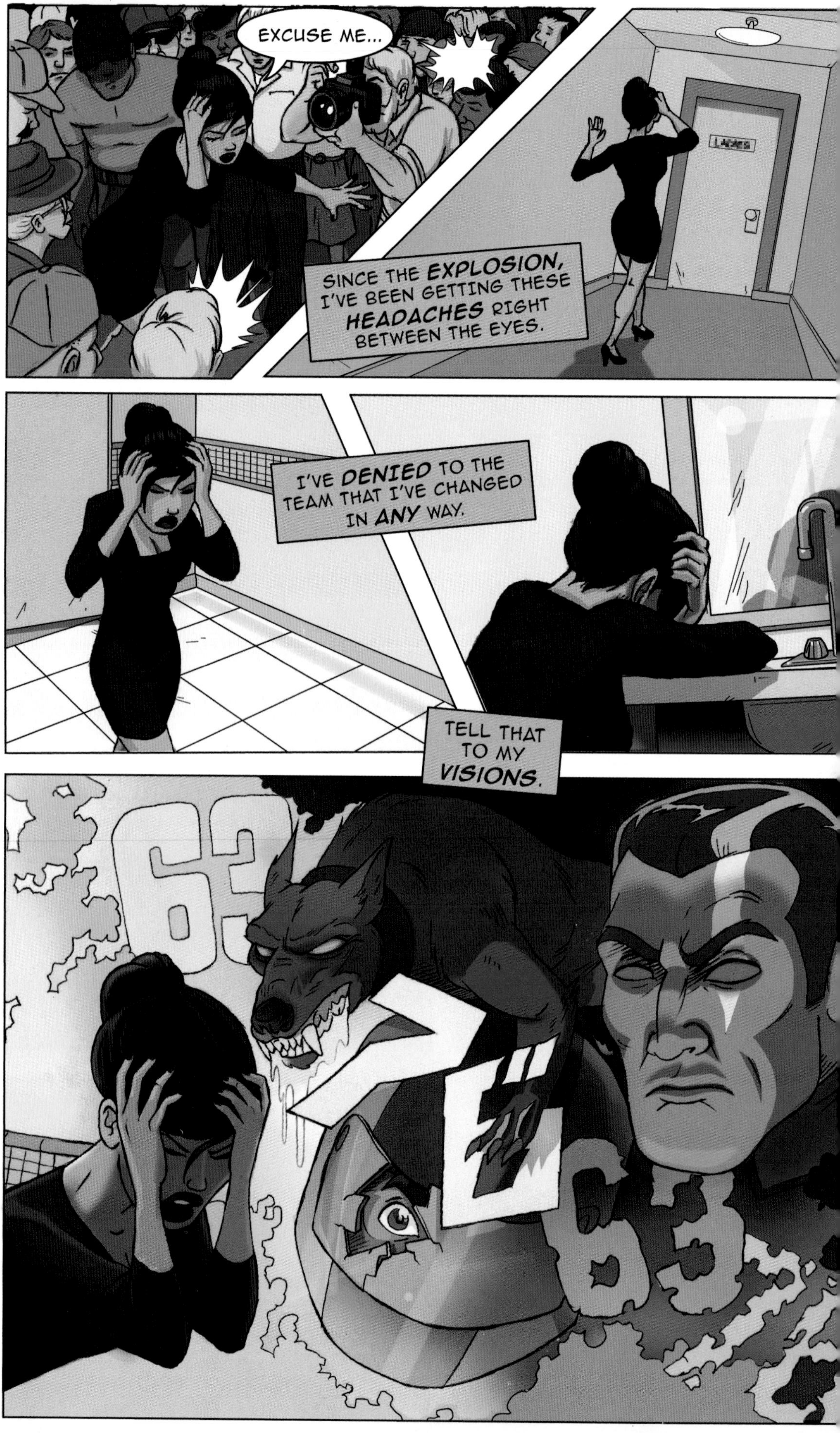
EXCUSE ME...
SINCE THE EXPLOSION, I'VE BEEN GETTING THESE HEADACHES RIGHT BETWEEN THE EYES.
LADIES
I'VE DENIED TO THE TEAM THAT I'VE CHANGED IN ANY WAY.
TELL THAT TO MY VISIONS.
63
63

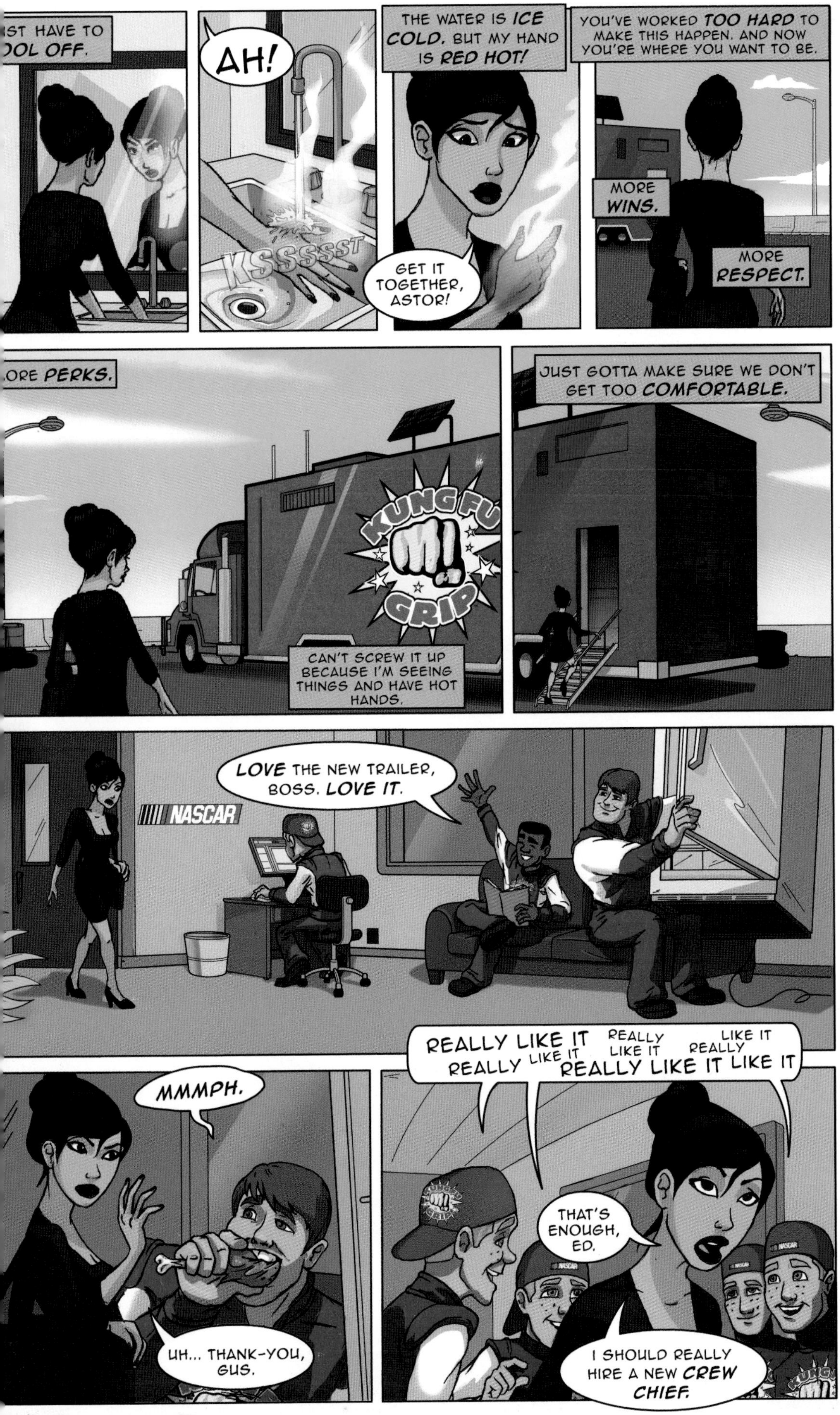
ST HAVE TO
OOL OFF.
AH!
KSSSSSST
THE WATER IS ICE COLD. BUT MY HAND IS RED HOT!
GET IT TOGETHER, ASTOR!
YOU'VE WORKED TOO HARD TO MAKE THIS HAPPEN. AND NOW YOU'RE WHERE YOU WANT TO BE.
MORE WINS.
MORE RESPECT.
ORE PERKS.
KUNG FU GRIP
CAN'T SCREW IT UP BECAUSE I'M SEEING THINGS AND HAVE HOT HANDS.
JUST GOTTA MAKE SURE WE DON'T GET TOO COMFORTABLE.
NASCAR
LOVE THE NEW TRAILER, BOSS. LOVE IT.
MMMPH.
UH... THANK-YOU, GUS.
REALLY LIKE IT REALLY LIKE IT REALLY LIKE IT LIKE IT REALLY LIKE IT REALLY LIKE IT LIKE IT
THAT'S ENOUGH, ED.
I SHOULD REALLY HIRE A NEW CREW CHIEF.

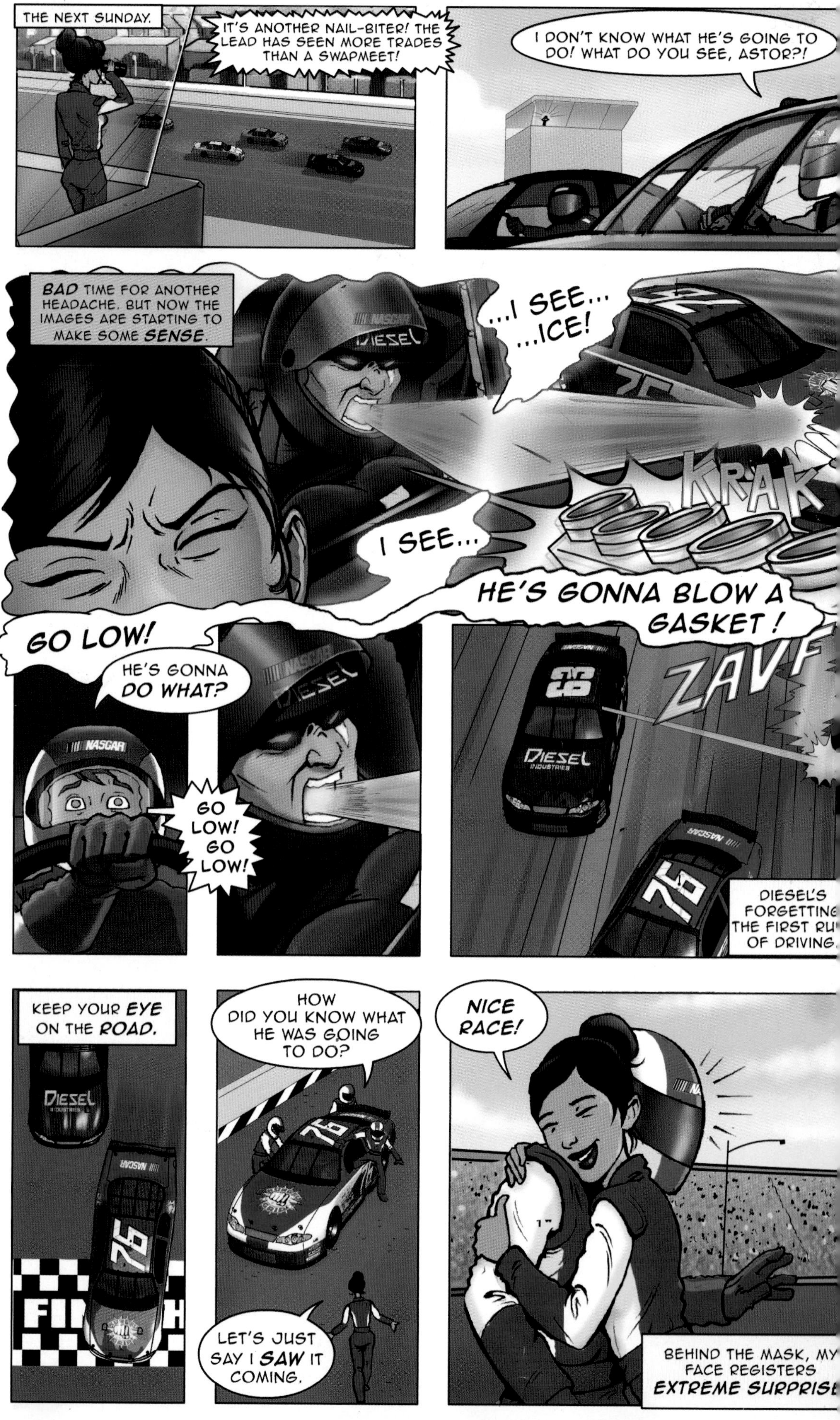
THE NEXT SUNDAY.
IT'S ANOTHER NAIL-BITER! THE LEAD HAS SEEN MORE TRADES THAN A SWAPMEET!
I DON'T KNOW WHAT HE'S GOING TO DO! WHAT DO YOU SEE, ASTOR?!
BAD TIME FOR ANOTHER HEADACHE. BUT NOW THE IMAGES ARE STARTING TO MAKE SOME SENSE.
NASCAR
DIESEL
...I SEE... ...ICE!
KRAK
I SEE...
HE'S GONNA BLOW A GASKET!
GO LOW!
HE'S GONNA DO WHAT?
NASCAR
GO LOW! GO LOW!
ZAVF
DIESEL INDUSTRIES
DIESEL'S FORGETTING THE FIRST RU OF DRIVING.
KEEP YOUR EYE ON THE ROAD.
DIESEL INDUSTRIES
NASCAR
FI H
HOW DID YOU KNOW WHAT HE WAS GOING TO DO?
LET'S JUST SAY I SAW IT COMING.
NICE RACE!
BEHIND THE MASK, MY FACE REGISTERS EXTREME SURPRISE

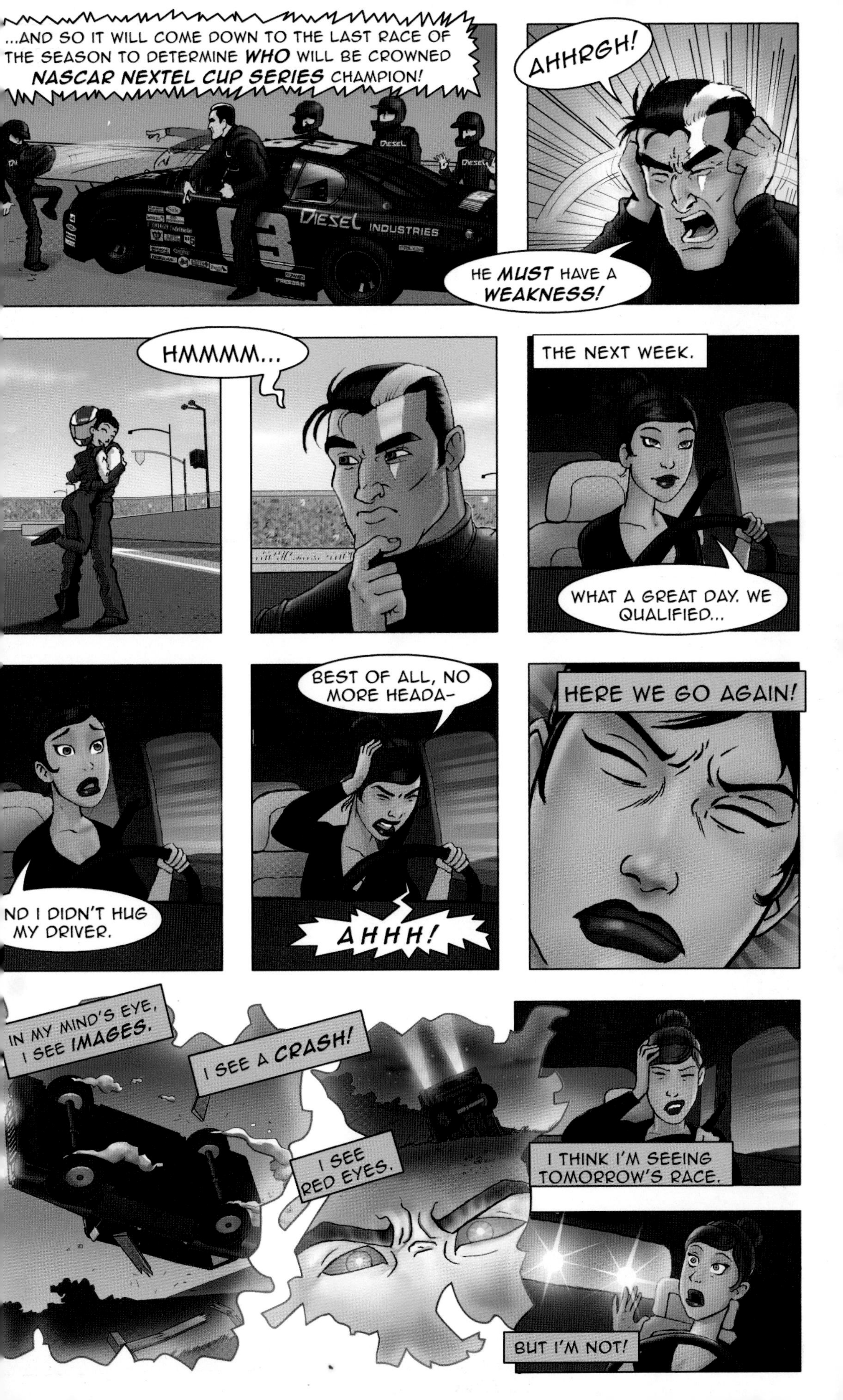
...AND SO IT WILL COME DOWN TO THE LAST RACE OF THE SEASON TO DETERMINE WHO WILL BE CROWNED NASCAR NEXTEL CUP SERIES CHAMPION!
DIESEL INDUSTRIES
AHHRGH!
HE MUST HAVE A WEAKNESS!
HMMMM...
THE NEXT WEEK.
WHAT A GREAT DAY. WE QUALIFIED...
AND I DIDN'T HUG MY DRIVER.
BEST OF ALL, NO MORE HEADA-
AHHH!
HERE WE GO AGAIN!
IN MY MIND'S EYE, I SEE IMAGES.
I SEE A CRASH!
I SEE RED EYES.
I THINK I'M SEEING TOMORROW'S RACE.
BUT I'M NOT!

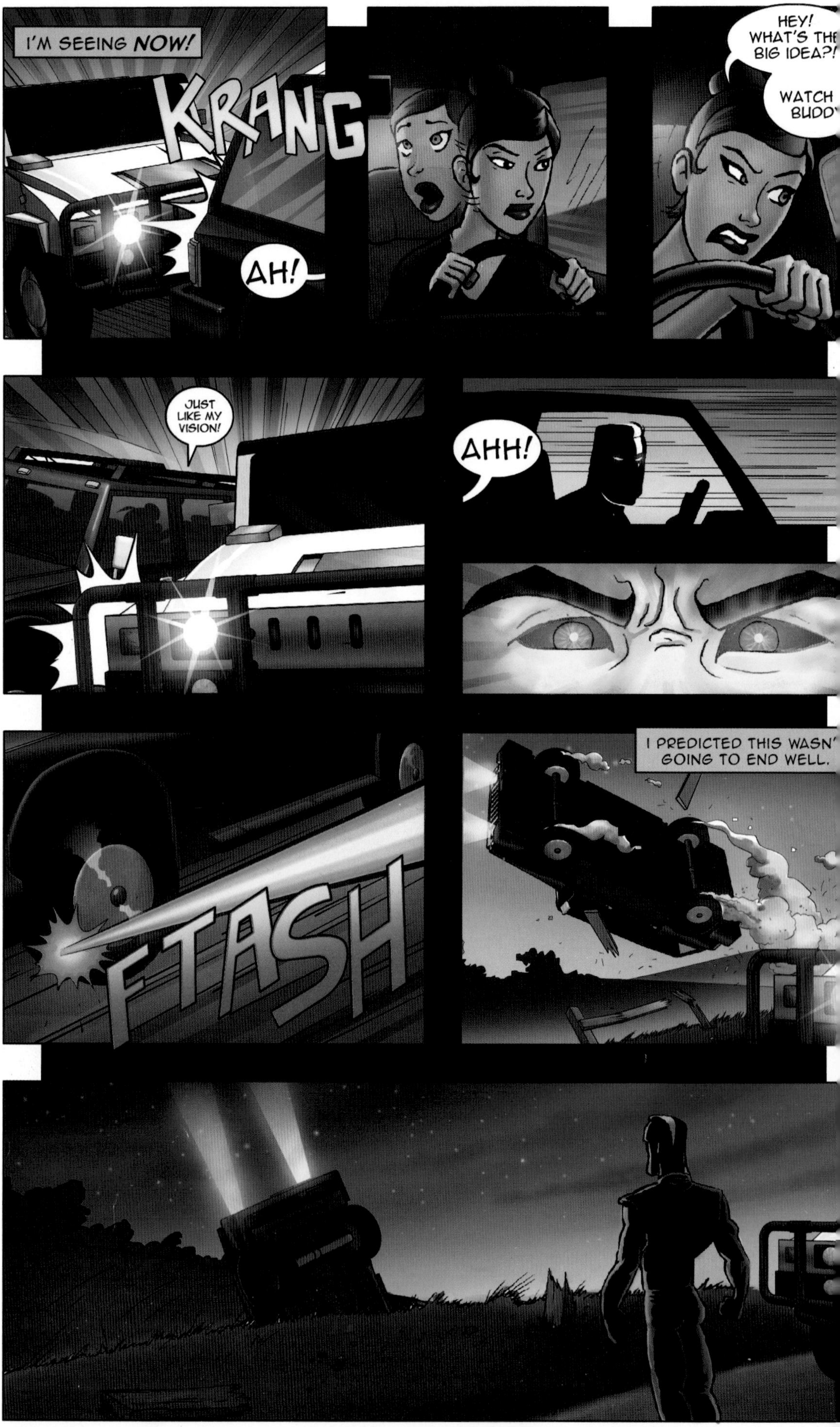
I'M SEEING NOW!
KRANG
AH!
HEY! WHAT'S THE BIG IDEA?!
WATCH BUDD
JUST LIKE MY VISION!
AHH!
FTASH
I PREDICTED THIS WASN' GOING TO END WELL.

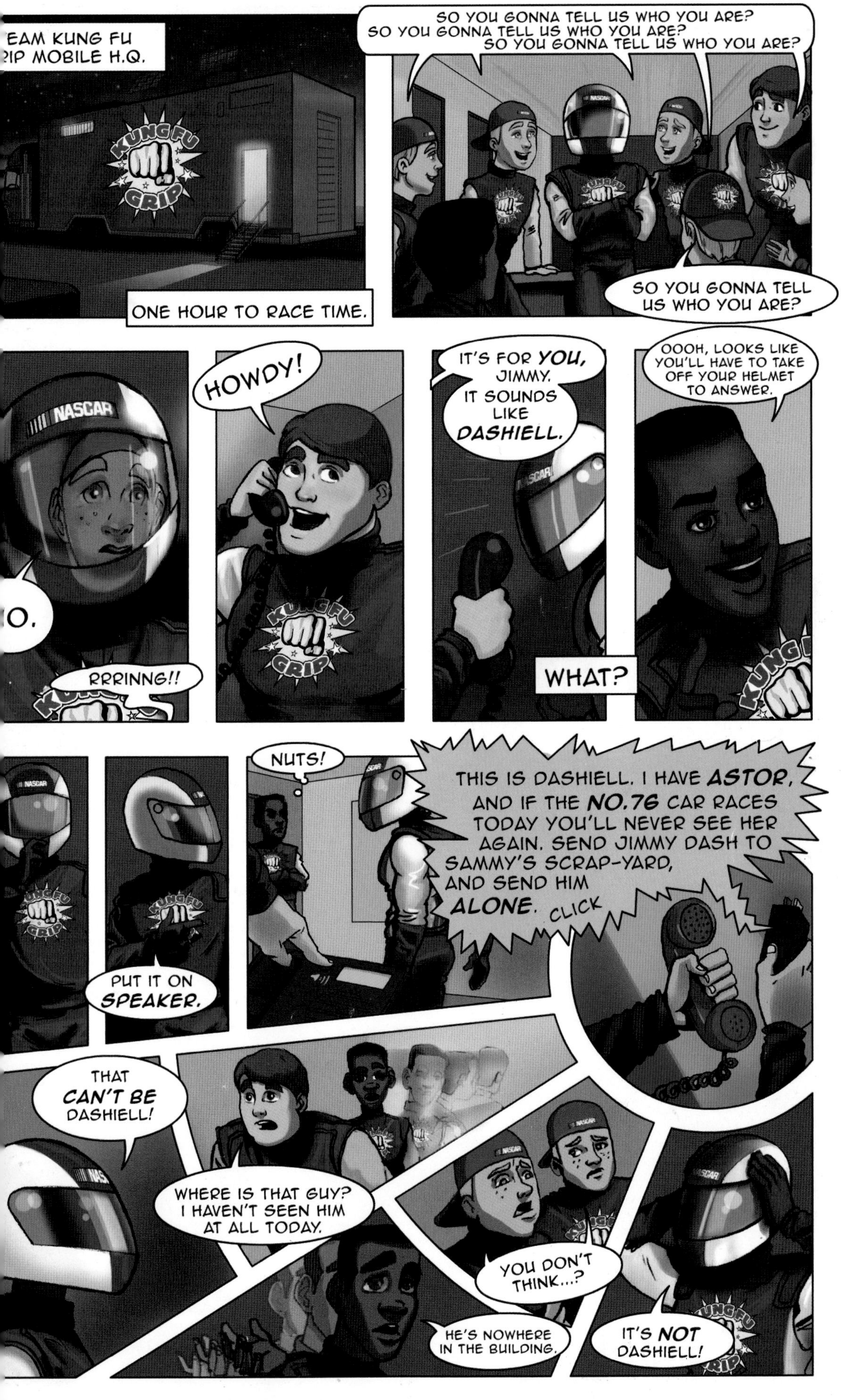
EAM KUNG FU
RIP MOBILE H.Q.
ONE HOUR TO RACE TIME.
SO YOU GONNA TELL US WHO YOU ARE?
SO YOU GONNA TELL US WHO YOU ARE?
SO YOU GONNA TELL US WHO YOU ARE?
SO YOU GONNA TELL US WHO YOU ARE?
O.
RRRINNG!!
HOWDY!
IT'S FOR YOU, JIMMY. IT SOUNDS LIKE DASHIELL.
WHAT?
OOOH, LOOKS LIKE YOU'LL HAVE TO TAKE OFF YOUR HELMET TO ANSWER.
PUT IT ON SPEAKER.
NUTS!
THIS IS DASHIELL. I HAVE ASTOR, AND IF THE NO.76 CAR RACES TODAY YOU'LL NEVER SEE HER AGAIN. SEND JIMMY DASH TO SAMMY'S SCRAP-YARD, AND SEND HIM ALONE. CLICK
THAT CAN'T BE DASHIELL!
WHERE IS THAT GUY? I HAVEN'T SEEN HIM AT ALL TODAY.
YOU DON'T THINK...?
HE'S NOWHERE IN THE BUILDING.
IT'S NOT DASHIELL!

PSYCHE.

I DON'T BELIEVE IT!

COOL!

SO WHAT HAPPENED TO *JIMMY DASH?*

WOW. YOU LOOK *GOOD* WITHOUT GLASSES.

SO, WHAT DO YOU THINK, DASH?

THERE'S ONLY ONE THING *TO* THINK.

DIESEL!

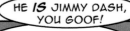

HE *IS* JIMMY DASH, YOU GOOF!

PROBABLY TRYING TO GET ME OUT OF THE RACE AND *PIN* IT ON *THE LITTLE GUY.* ALSO ME. LET'S GO!

BUT HE SAID YOU SHOULD GO *ALONE!*

HEY— WHERE I GO, MY *TEAM* GOES.

WHO'S DRIVING?

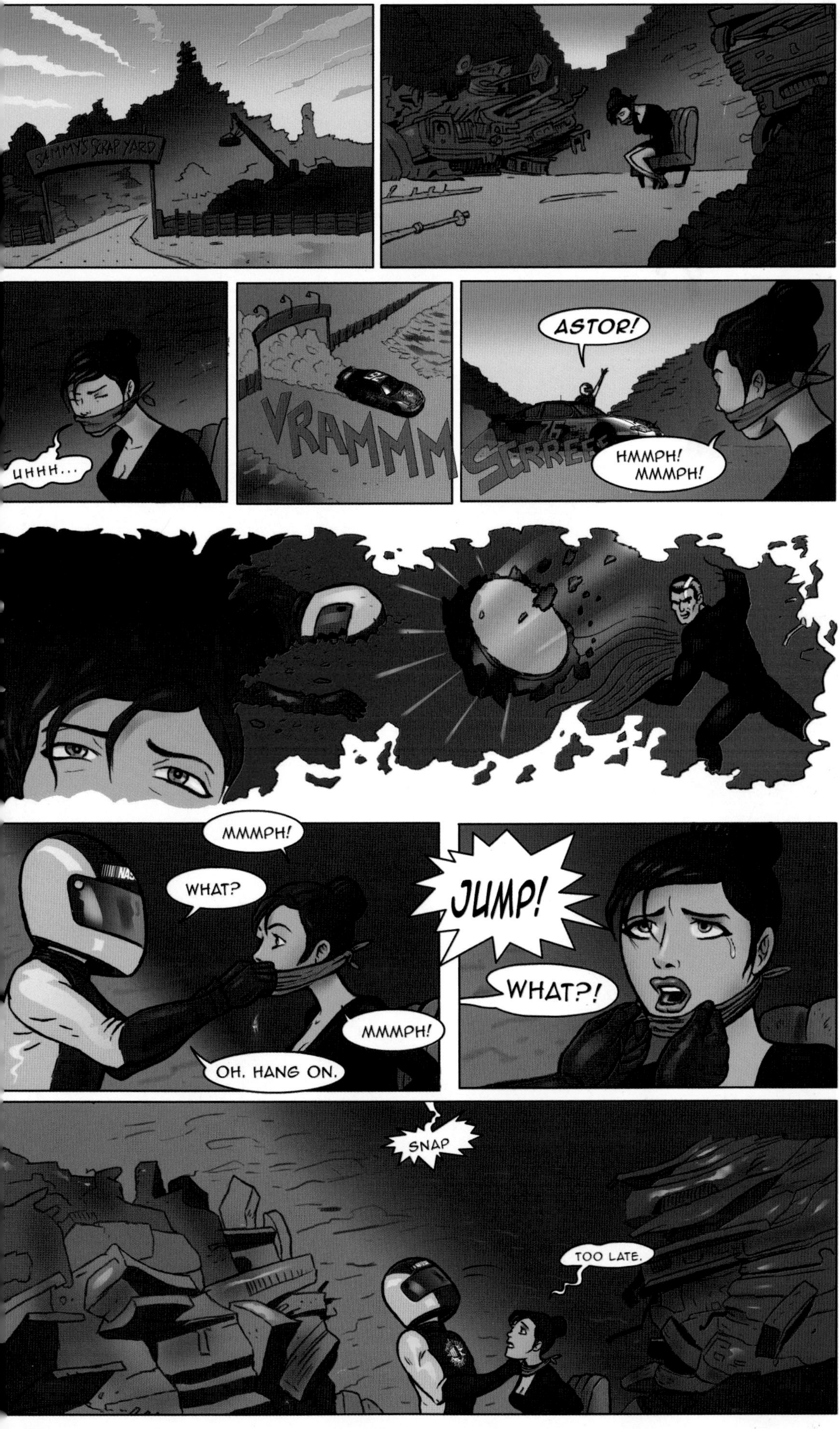
SAMMY'S SCRAP YARD
UHHH...
VRAMMM
ASTOR!
SCREEE
HMMPH! MMMPH!
MMMPH!
WHAT?
MMMPH!
OH. HANG ON.
JUMP!
WHAT?!
SNAP
TOO LATE.

WUMP!
KLANG
KRANG
KLUKRANG
THAT OUGHT TO STUN HIM.
STUN HIM? HE'S DEAD!
OH, HE'S NOT DEAD
NO.
...BUT IN THREE SECONDS YOU'RE GOIN
TO WISH I WERE!!!

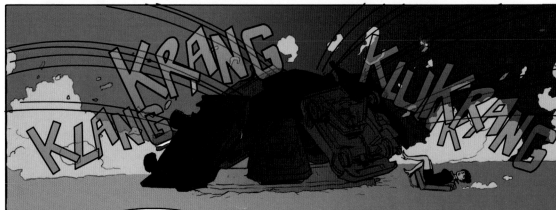

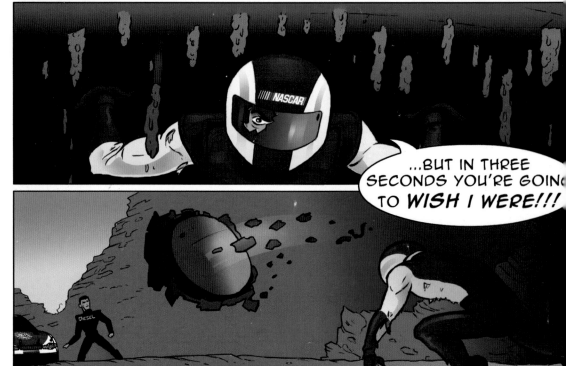

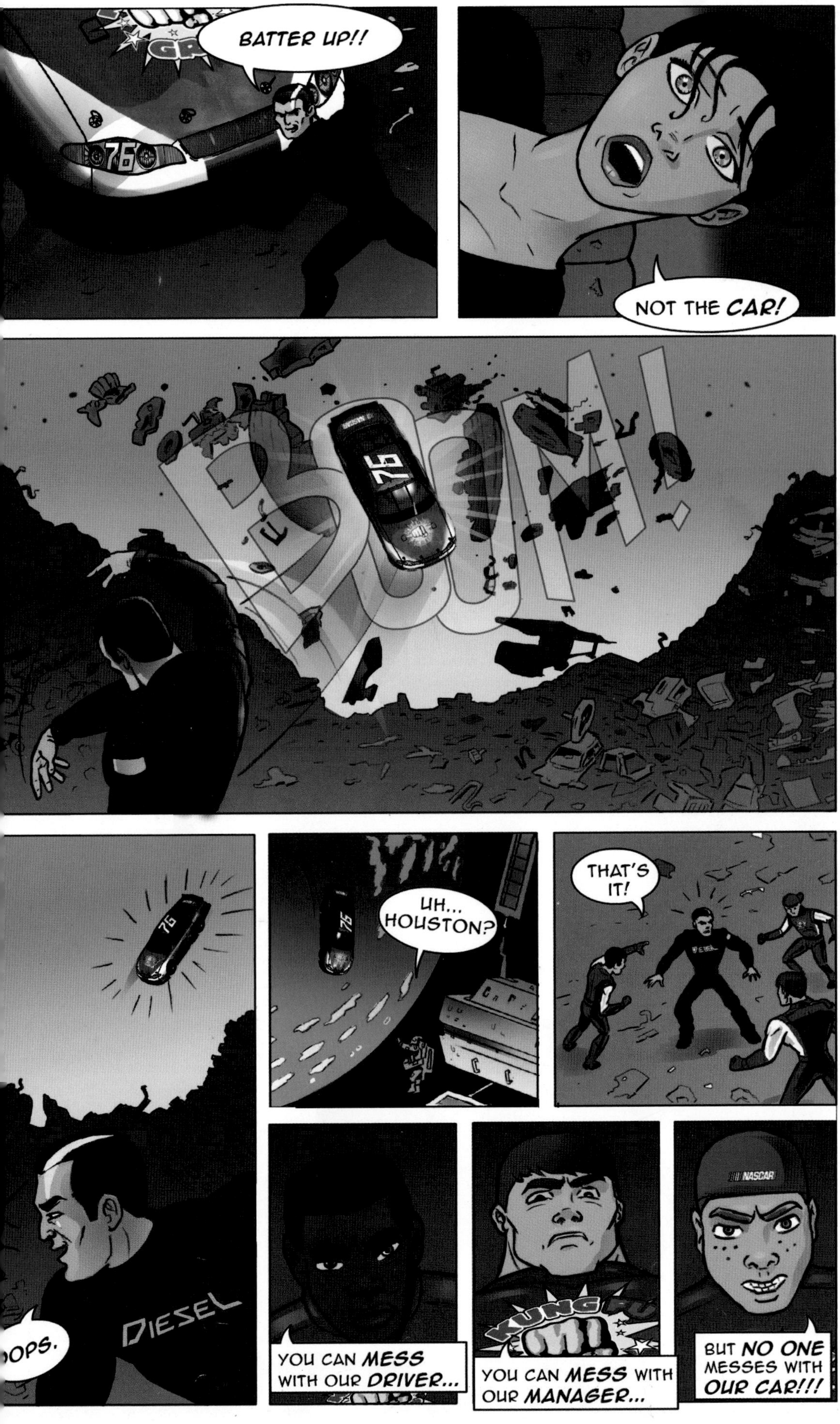
BATTER UP!!
NOT THE CAR!
UH... HOUSTON?
THAT'S IT!
OPS.
DIESEL
YOU CAN MESS WITH OUR DRIVER...
YOU CAN MESS WITH OUR MANAGER...
BUT NO ONE MESSES WITH OUR CAR!!!

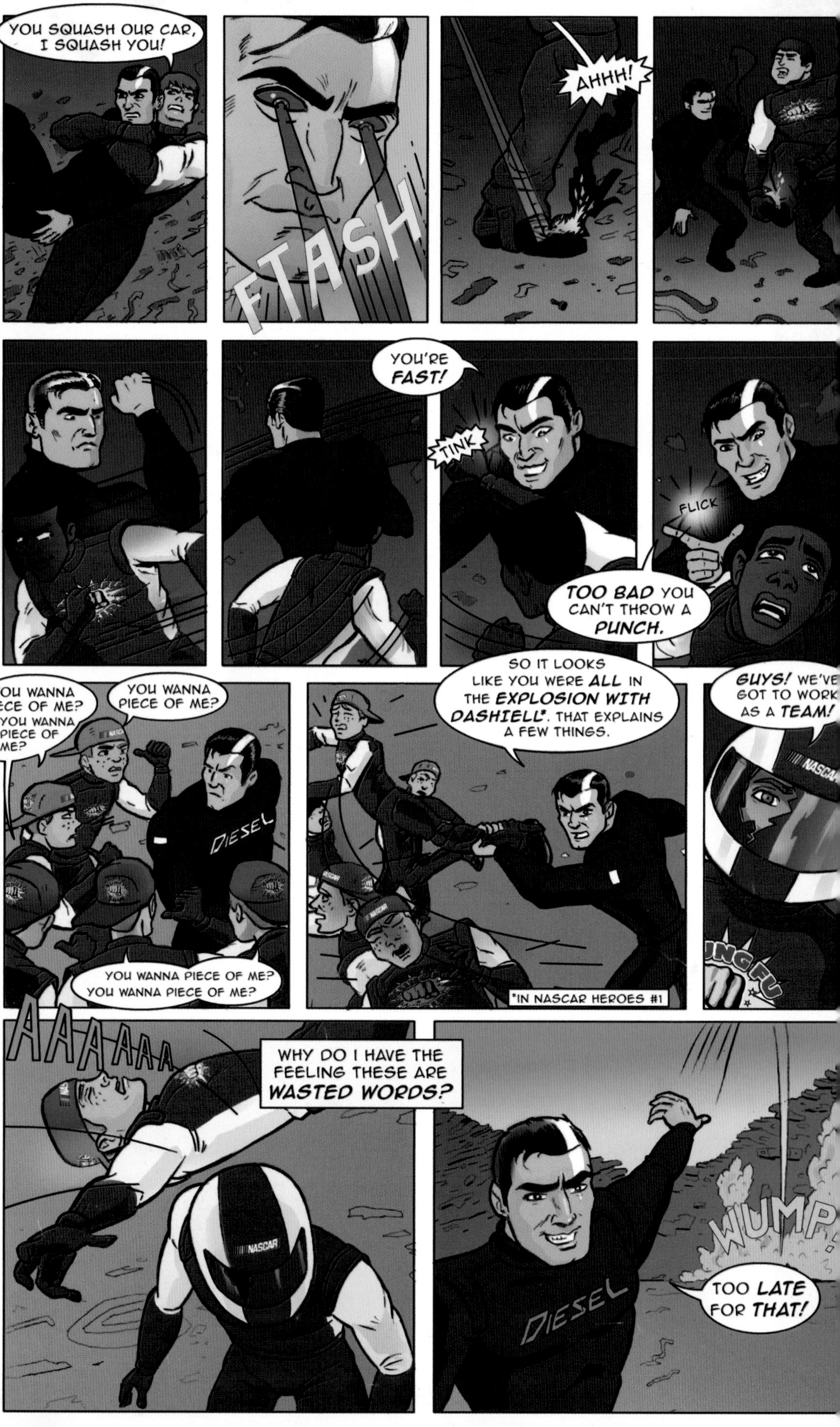
YOU SQUASH OUR CAR, I SQUASH YOU!
FTASH
AHHH!
YOU'RE FAST!
TINK
FLICK
TOO BAD YOU CAN'T THROW A PUNCH.
YOU WANNA PIECE OF ME? YOU WANNA PIECE OF ME?
YOU WANNA PIECE OF ME?
NASCAR
DIESEL
YOU WANNA PIECE OF ME? YOU WANNA PIECE OF ME?
SO IT LOOKS LIKE YOU WERE ALL IN THE EXPLOSION WITH DASHIELL*. THAT EXPLAINS A FEW THINGS.
*IN NASCAR HEROES #1
GUYS! WE'VE GOT TO WORK AS A TEAM!
AAAAAAA
WHY DO I HAVE THE FEELING THESE ARE WASTED WORDS?
NASCAR
WUMP
TOO LATE FOR THAT!
DIESEL

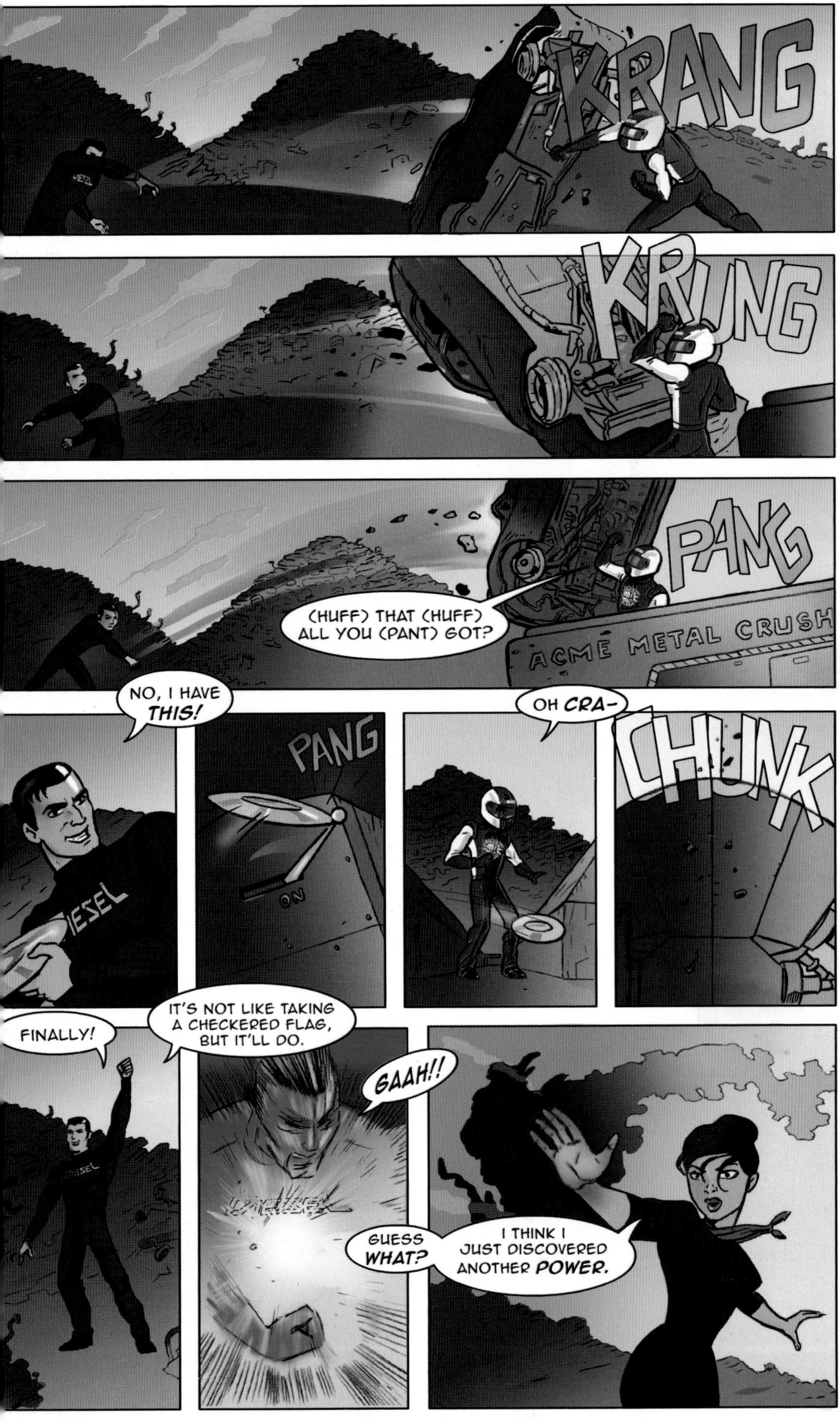
KRANG
KRUNG
PANG
(HUFF) THAT (HUFF) ALL YOU (PANT) GOT?
ACME METAL CRUSH
NO, I HAVE THIS!
PANG
ON
OH CRA-
CHUNK
FINALLY!
IT'S NOT LIKE TAKING A CHECKERED FLAG, BUT IT'LL DO.
GAAH!!
GUESS WHAT?
I THINK I JUST DISCOVERED ANOTHER POWER.

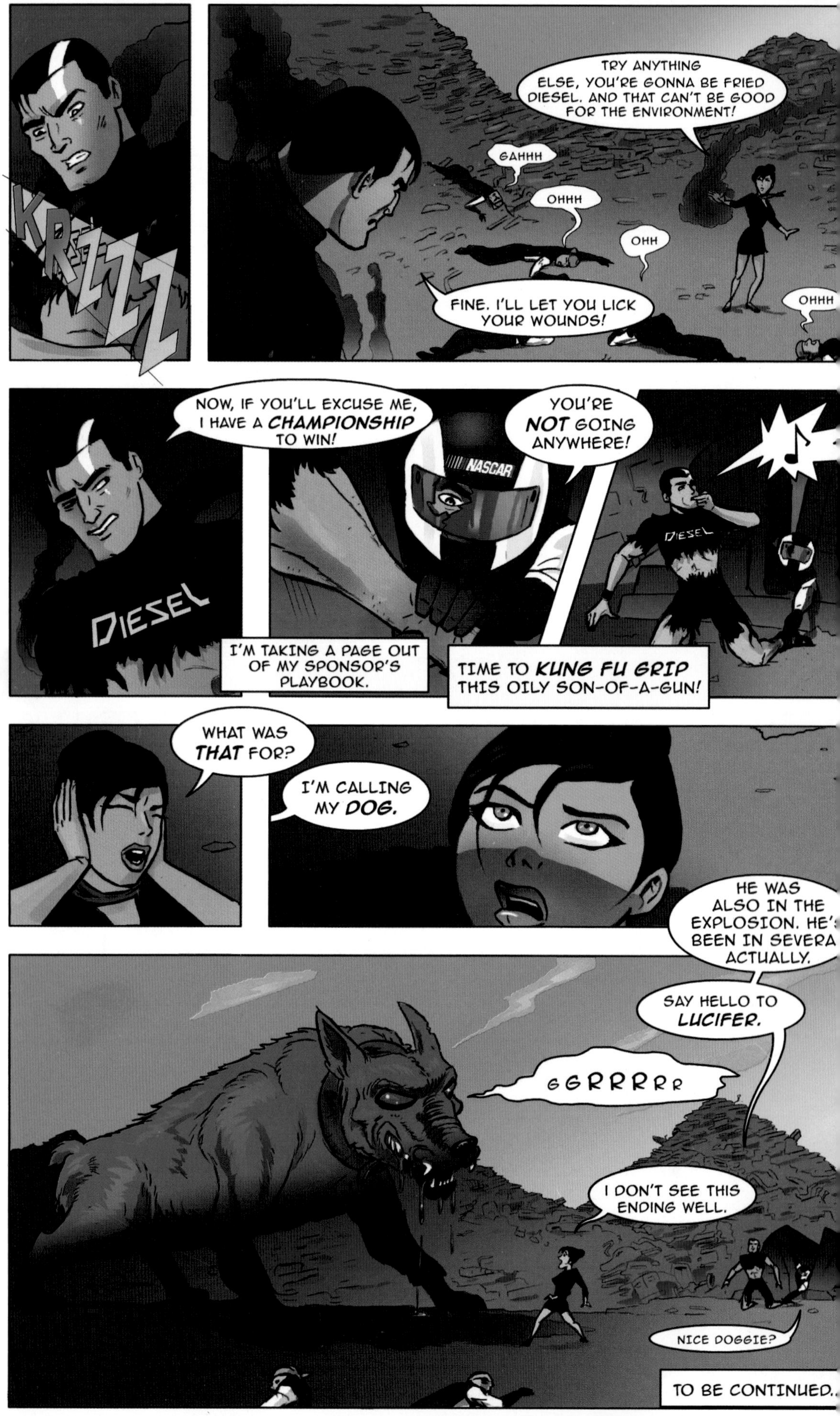
KRZZZZ
TRY ANYTHING ELSE, YOU'RE GONNA BE FRIED DIESEL. AND THAT CAN'T BE GOOD FOR THE ENVIRONMENT!
GAHHH
OHHH
OHH
OHHH
FINE. I'LL LET YOU LICK YOUR WOUNDS!
NOW, IF YOU'LL EXCUSE ME, I HAVE A CHAMPIONSHIP TO WIN!
NASCAR
YOU'RE NOT GOING ANYWHERE!
DIESEL
DIESEL
I'M TAKING A PAGE OUT OF MY SPONSOR'S PLAYBOOK.
TIME TO KUNG FU GRIP THIS OILY SON-OF-A-GUN!
WHAT WAS THAT FOR?
I'M CALLING MY DOG.
HE WAS ALSO IN THE EXPLOSION. HE'S BEEN IN SEVERA ACTUALLY.
SAY HELLO TO LUCIFER.
GGRRRRRR
I DON'T SEE THIS ENDING WELL.
NICE DOGGIE?
TO BE CONTINUED...

HOW TO DRAW JIMMY DASH

NASCAR COMICS

BY JOHN GALLAGHER

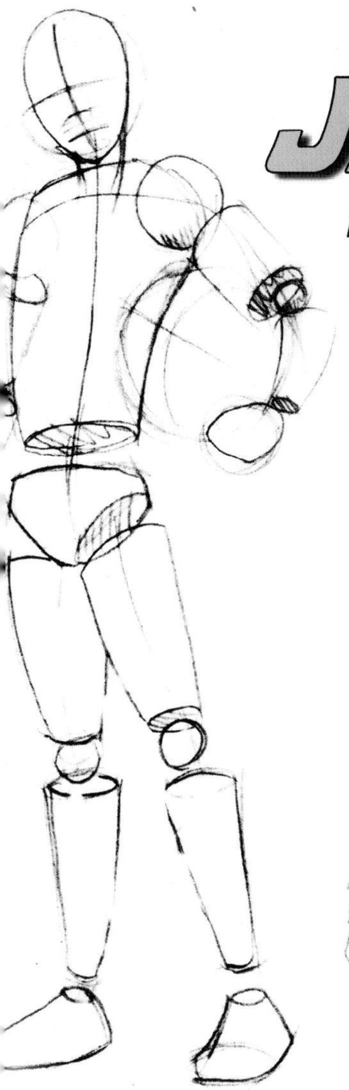

STEP 1: USING A PENCIL, BEGIN WITH A SIMPLE FRAMEWORK. A STICK FIGURE WILL DO THE TRICK TO START! ADD CIRCLES, OVALS AND CYLINDERS TO FLESH OUT THE FIGURE. SIMPLE SHAPES ARE THE BUILDING BLOCKS OF ANY GREAT SUPER HERO (AND SUPER STRENGTH AND SPEED HELP, TOO!).

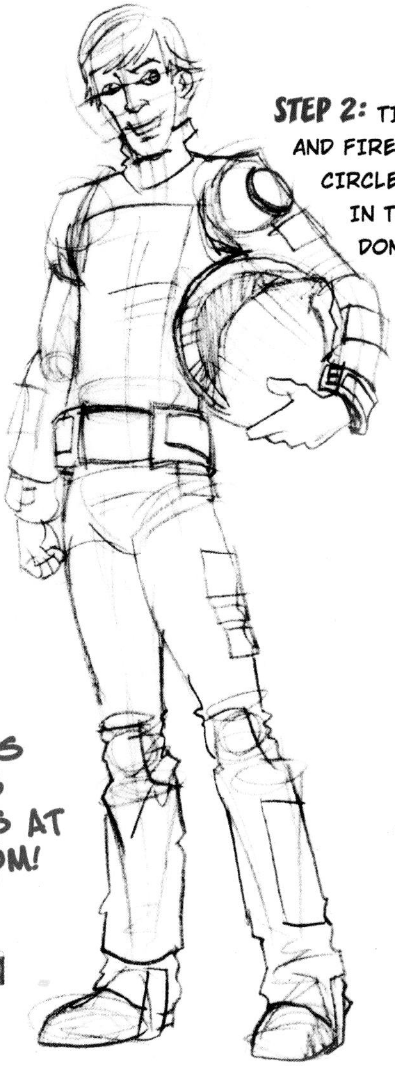

STEP 2: TIME TO FLESH OUT JIMMY'S BODY AND FIRE SUIT. USE GUIDELINES TO ADD CIRCLES FOR HIS EYES. START FILLING IN THE HAIR, AND CLOTHING, AND DON'T FORGET THE HELMET!

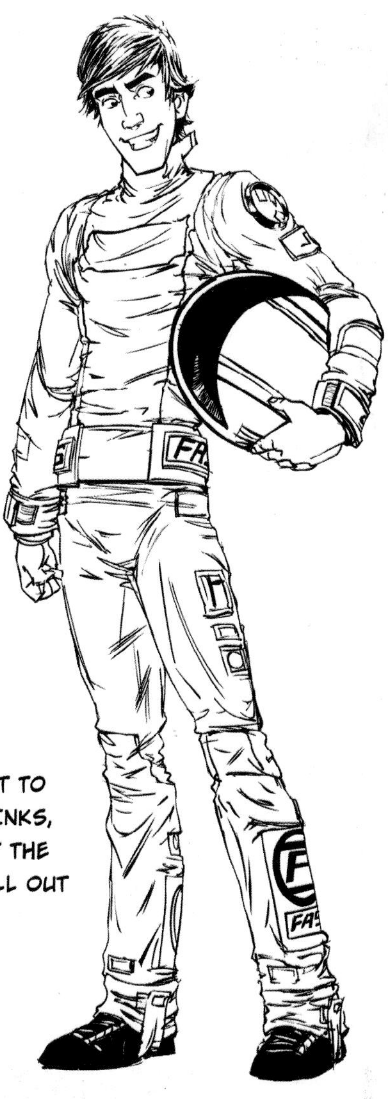

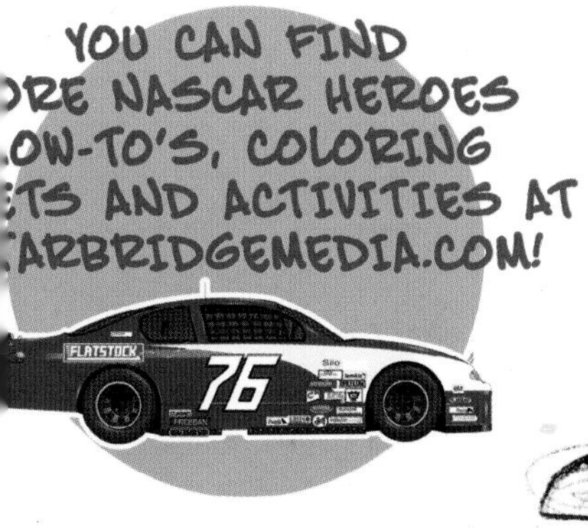
YOU CAN FIND
ORE NASCAR HEROES
OW-TO'S, COLORING
TS AND ACTIVITIES AT
ARBRIDGEMEDIA.COM!
FLATSTOCK
76

STEP 3: AT THIS POINT, YOU CAN GO IN WITH A PEN AND START TO INK THE FIGURE. ERASE THE PENCIL LINES UNDERNEATH THE INKS, FIXING ANY MISTAKES IN YOUR DRAWINGS. REMEMBER TO LET THE PEN INK DRY BEFORE ERASING, TO AVOID SMUDGES! NOW, PULL OUT YOUR MARKERS OR CRAYONS, AND ADD SOME COLOR!

NASCAR LIBRARY COLLECTION

NASCAR HEROES

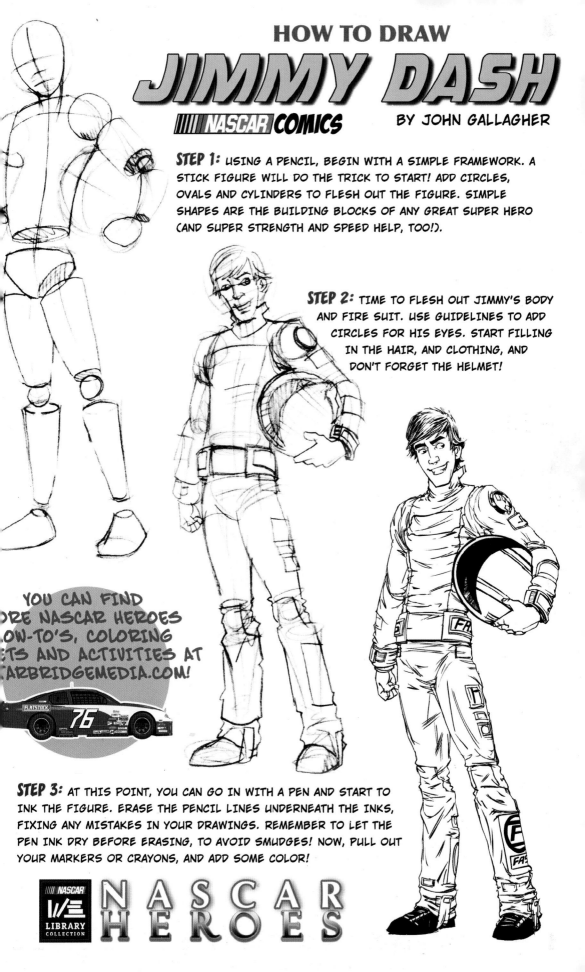

HOW TO DRAW NASCAR COMICS
JACK DIESEL'S NO. 63

BY JOHN GALLAGHER

SURE, JACK DIESEL'S A BAD GUY, BUT HE'S GOT A SET OF WHEELS THAT MAKE HIM A NASCAR SUPERSTAR! HERE'S A QUICK GUIDE ON HOW YOU CAN DRAW JACK'S RIDE!

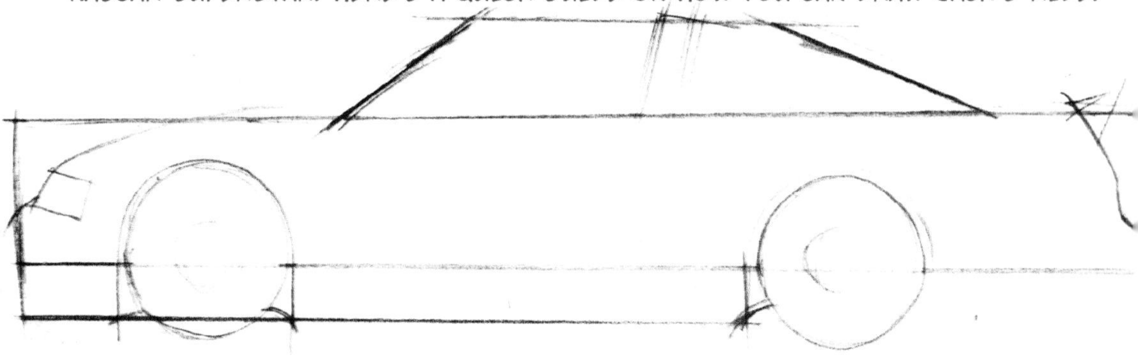

STEP 1: START OFF BY DRAWING A SERIES OF BOXES, SUGGESTING THE SHAPE OF THE CAR AND TIRES. IT'S LIKE CREATING A SHAPE WITH BUILDING BLOCKS, THEN CARVING AWAY AT THE SHAPE INSIDE. YOU CAN DO THIS FREEHAND, OR WITH A RULER, DEPENDING ON HOW "TIGHT" YOU WANT YOUR DRAWING!

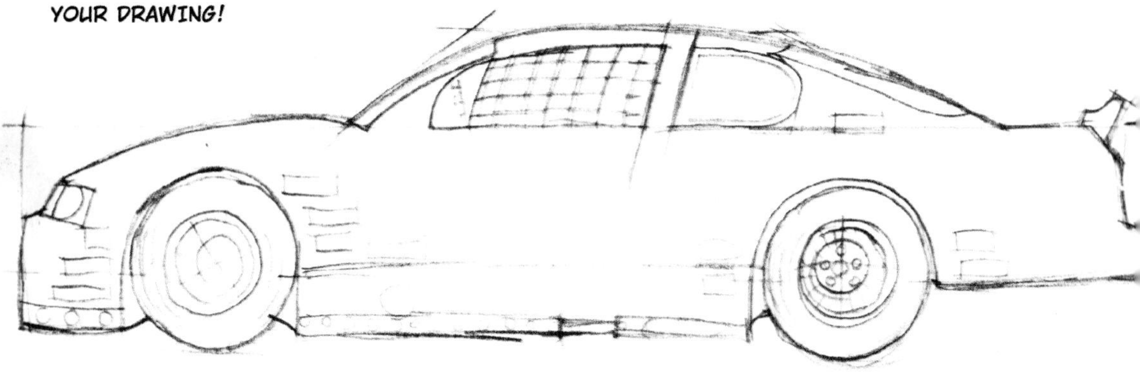

STEP 2: NOW, START TO ZERO IN ON THE SHAPE OF THE CAR FRONT, WINDOWS, TIRES, AND REAR SPOILER. THEN, YOU'LL WANT TO ADD THE DETAILS THAT MAKE A NASCAR UNIQUE, LIKE DECALS, NUMBERS, AND RIVETS!

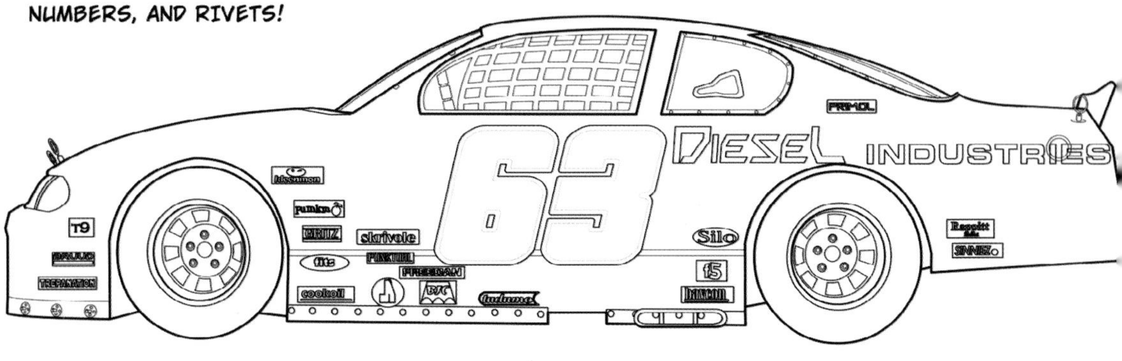
63
DIESEL
INDUSTRIES
Silo
T9
skrivole
cookoil

STEP 3: AT THIS POINT, YOU CAN GO IN WITH A PEN AND START TO INK THE CAR, REALLY SHARPENING THE IMAGE! ERASE THE PENCIL LINES UNDERNEATH THE INKS, FIXING ANY MISTAKES IN YOUR DRAWING. GIVE THE CAR THE NUMBER OF YOUR FAVORITE DRIVE (BUT DON'T TELL JACK!), AND ADD SOME COLOR! NOW YOUR DRAWING IS READY TO RACE!

NASCAR LIBRARY COLLECTION

NASCAR HEROES

YOU CAN FIND MORE NASCAR HEROES HOW-TO'S, COLORING SHEETS AND ACTIVITIES STARBRIDGEMEDIA.CO

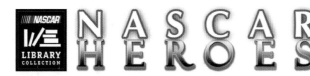